## "I want you to be my wife."

She stared at him, completely stunned. "You're kidding or you're mental," she grated.

"No, just logical. My father is ill. His last few months will be much easier if he knows I am married."

"But why me?" she asked almost silently. It did not make sense. Xavier was the kind of man who could get any woman he chose. He certainly did not need to blackmail a woman into marrying him.

"I want a mutually beneficial arrangement with no sentimental strings attached. A woman to warm my bed, without pretending to warm my heart. Knowing you as I do, that makes you the perfect candidate."

His casual arrogance fed her rage. "Go to hell! And take your asinine proposal with you!" She would not dignify it with an answer, but beneath her anger there was a growing sense of fear.

He laughed harshly. "I may go to hell, but believe me, I'm taking you with me. You owe me, and I always collect on my debts."

# Jacqueline Baird

# A MOST PASSIONATE REVENGE

## Passion™

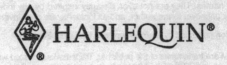

ISBN 0-373-12137-7

A MOST PASSIONATE REVENGE

First North American Publication 2000.

Copyright © 2000 by Jacqueline Baird.

Visit us at www.eHarlequin.com

**Printed in U.S.A.**

# CHAPTER ONE

'THE BOY is only twenty-four years old; that's far too young to marry. Jamie is your son; surely you can talk him out of it?' Xavier demanded, with a cynical twist to his sensual mouth as he glanced down at his sister, Teresa, lounging on the sofa. He knew from personal experience his older sister was perfectly capable of controlling her son, if she wanted to. *¡Dios!* She'd certainly controlled Xavier when their mother had died when he was only eight. Ten years older than him she'd taken on the role of mother and had been stricter than the mother they'd lost. Much as he loved his sister, he had heaved a sigh of relief when at the age of twenty-four Teresa had met and fallen in love with David Easterby. The Englishman had been visiting their ranch some miles east of Seville to purchase a pure Spanish-Andaluz horse, for his stables in Yorkshire.

The rest was history, Xavier mused. Twenty-five years on their only child wanted to get married. The reason for his trip to the farm and racing stables in the heart of the Yorkshire Dales was to attend a dinner party for the engaged couple, at a nearby country house hotel, arranged so the two families could meet. Xavier was a reluctant guest…

'Your trouble is that you have never been in love.' Teresa's comment interrupted his thoughts.

'But I have been married,' Xavier drawled mockingly. 'And I can assure you Teresa, very few people in this world find the kind of partnership you and David share.'

'Rubbish, you're just a hopeless cynic,' his sister responded bluntly. 'Anyway it's Jamie's decision and David

5

and I support him unconditionally. They will be here any minute, so please keep your opinions to yourself, and try to be civil to his fiancée Ann, and her parents.'

'Not to mention the spinster cousin,' Xavier prompted with the sardonic arch of one ebony brow. He'd been disconcerted to learn on his arrival three hours earlier that not only were the parents and the fiancée staying for the weekend, but also a female cousin. 'I'm warning you, Teresa; if you have any notion of pairing me off with the lady—forget it!'

'As if I would dare!' Teresa said archly, her dark eyes sweeping over his six feet four frame and comparing it with her own very average build. Her brother was a formidable man in every respect; wealthy, powerful and with a spectacularly handsome profile, night black hair, and hooded chestnut brown eyes that appeared almost golden when he was amused or excited. As a young man, women had fallen at his feet like ninepins and he'd taken full advantage of the fact. But for the past few years the gold was rarely evident in his gaze. His eyes were cold and hard, and he rarely smiled. 'I doubt anyone would dare challenge you anymore, Xavier, about anything,' Teresa added a flicker of compassion in her brown eyes.

Wincing at the unwanted pity he saw in his sister's face, Xavier gave her an exasperated glance then turned and crossed the elegant yet comfortable living room. After all it was none of his business. If his nephew wanted to get married at a ridiculously young age why should he try to stop him? He stood in the large bow of the window and gazed out over the gravelled drive and parkland beyond, without really seeing it. His thoughts were on his father, Don Pablo Ortega Valdespino. At seventy-nine and with a weak heart he was too ill to travel to England and so he'd insisted on Xavier representing him at the engagement party.

Xavier and his father rarely saw eye to eye on anything, and Jamie's forthcoming betrothal had been no exception. It was only when Don Pablo had begun berating him for not producing children of his own to carry on the family name that Xavier had given in, and agreed to be his father's representative for the weekend. He disliked house parties unless they were in his own home with a few carefully chosen friends. In fact it must be almost nine years since he'd spent a weekend out of Spain on anything other than business. Xavier supposed it was time to face up to the fact that he'd become jaded. His work was his life, with an occasional visit to his mistress to take care of his physical needs, and thinking back it must be over five months since he'd even done that….

The sound of a car caught his attention, and he stared through the window with some interest at the two vehicles coming up the drive. He recognised the first one as the large four-wheel drive that belonged to Jamie. He should, he'd bought it for the boy as a twenty-first birthday present. But it was the second that grabbed his attention. It was a classic racing green E-Type Jaguar of the nineteen sixties. The exaggerated long elegant bonnet and wire wheels were un-mistakable and with the bodywork gleaming in the after-noon sun, it was immaculate; a delight to any dedicated car buff, and Xavier did love cars.

His nephew, Jamie, bounced out of the first vehicle, and opened the rear door, allowing a middle-aged couple to alight. Xavier glanced briefly at the man and the woman, and at the pretty brunette who'd appeared at Jamie's side, the bride-to-be presumably. But it was the second car that held his attention. The weekend might not be lost after all, with a bit of luck he could talk cars to a real enthusiast.

The owner of the E-Type Jaguar was obviously a person after his own heart.

Xavier tensed. His hooded dark eyes—usually so cold—suddenly flared with a brilliant light, as the driver alighted and rubbed a microscopic speck of dust from the front wing. It was a woman, and *what* a woman! Tall, long-legged, Titian hair scraped back from her face and tied at her nape with a red silk scarf. She turned towards the boot of the car and he saw the tumble of curls reached halfway down her elegant back. The voices floated up on the cool spring air and Xavier's dark brows drew together in a thunderous frown.

'Where on earth did this old wreck of a car come from, Rose? It can't possibly be environmentally-friendly!' Jamie demanded, but amusement danced in his eyes and his arm was firmly fixed around the waist of his fiancée, which softened his scathing comments.

The driver slammed the trunk closed, and with a week-end case in one hand she tilted back her head, and glanced across at the young couple. 'Watch it, boyoh! Any one who insults Bertram insults *moi!* He's the love of my life and far more dependable than any man.' Brilliant green eyes sparkled with amusement, and a lush mouth curved in a broad smile as the stunning woman strode over to the young couple.

'And for your information, Jamie, it came from my father; it was his pride and joy, and is probably worth twice as much as that monster motor you drive.'

'She's right. It's a classic and highly sought after,' the older grey-haired man cut in and turned to the woman. 'A bit of a coincidence meeting on the road like that! I hope you didn't drive too fast, Rosalyn dear.'

'Yes it was quite a coincidence. I recognised Jamie's car just outside of Richmond, but then I had the dubious pleasure of being picked up by these two at the airport last week. And no, Uncle Alex, I never broke the speed limit all the way here,' she laughed.

Xavier hardly heard the conversation. The instant tightening in his groin had been a stunning affirmation of the woman's beauty. '*¡Dios mío!*' he exclaimed under his breath. He'd never reacted this strongly to a woman in over a decade. He was shocked but not surprised. He'd just been thinking it was a long time since he'd visited his mistress!

He took a step back and half concealed by the velvet drapes at the window, he watched, his tall broad-shouldered frame rigid with tension. His dark eyes narrowed intently on the red-haired laughing woman and in that instant his decision was made. He was going to have her. He was going to crush those pouting sensual lips beneath his own. He was going to strip that delicious body naked and bury himself in her womanhood over and over again. A devilish light of challenge burned in his deep brown eyes; he felt more vitally alive than he had in years. The weekend promised to be an experience he would never forget, and neither would the laughing woman, he vowed. He felt like punching his nephew simply because she bestowed a smile upon the young man.

He saw her glance up at the window and suddenly realising what he was doing, he shoved his hands deep into the pockets of his black jeans. Her fate was sealed but now was not the time, not yet... He needed a game plan, and at the moment his hands were shaking and his brain was clouded by testosterone, just like a hormonal teenager.

He spun around. 'Your guests have arrived, Teresa,' he said with not a hint of the turmoil in his mind showing in his hard expressionless face. 'I'm going for a walk; I'll meet them at dinner.' And, not waiting for a response, he strode across the room through the adjoining conservatory and out into the side garden of the house.

A SMILE lingering around her lips, Rose glanced up at the house. Built with small red bricks, and mellowed with time it looked friendly and welcoming. The graceful bay windows were surrounded with a profusion of climbing plants. The fresh bright green leaves of a Virginia creeper half covered the walls and intermingled with the small pink flowers of a rampant clematis. The weekend was looking better already. She smoothed her green cashmere sweater down over her slim hips, and tightening her grip on her weekend case she moved forward, then stopped and hesitated for a second before walking on.

Then she shivered; all the hair on her body leaped to attention and she had the inexplicable feeling that someone's eyes were following her every move. She glanced back up at the rambling building and for some reason it no longer seemed so friendly. Don't be stupid, she told herself, and quickened her pace to catch up with the others, heading for the front door.

The director of the overseas medical relief agency for whom she'd worked for the past three years had warned her that she badly needed a rest. She was becoming far too involved with her young patients, and was suffering from emotional fatigue. For these reasons he'd insisted she return to England for an extended three-month holiday, saying that otherwise she would crack up. She hadn't wanted to believe him but maybe he was right. If she was going to imagine that eyes were following her everywhere, she really needed the break!

The front door was opened wide, and Rose forgot her fears as she was swept up in a flurry of introductions. Jamie's mother, Teresa, was a small dark-haired, very attractive woman, somewhere in her forties. His father David was tall with grey hair and looked a good few years older than his wife.

Milling around in the large hall the conversation was typical: the weather, and the journey down. Rose glanced at her Aunt Jean and Uncle Alex, and was happy to see they seemed to be relaxed. Her cousin, Ann, was clasped to Jamie's side, as if he was frightened she would run away, and the glances the two youngsters shared told the world they were madly in love.

'My father was unable to travel all the way to Yorkshire from our family home in Seville because of ill health, but hopefully he will be better by the wedding in September,' Teresa explained, before offering to show them to their rooms.

*Seville!* Rose's heart missed a beat. 'You're Spanish! But you don't sound it—' she blurted, and colour surged up her face as the conversation stopped and everyone looked at her. Teresa laughed and broke the awkward moment.

'My husband is always telling me I sound more Yorkshire than he does, but I have lived here twenty-five years so it is hardly surprising.'

Not to Teresa maybe, but it was a hell of a shock to Rose and five minutes later as she followed everyone upstairs, she was still worrying. Uncle Alex and Aunt Jean disappeared into a bedroom suite at the front of the house, with Ann next door, and Rose continued along the hall with Teresa. Her hostess indicated a closed door with a wave of her hand.

'This is my brother's bedroom. He arrived this morning but he has gone for a walk on the moors. You will meet him at dinner.' Teresa led her to the next door. 'This is your room.'

Mechanically Rose made the right response and walked

into the bedroom. A brother! The news, coupled with the earlier mention of Seville sent alarm bells ringing in her mind. She shrugged her slender shoulders dismissing the chilling thought. There must be a million or more people in Seville. The odds on it being the only other Sevilliano she'd met must be astronomical.

Still, no one had said anything about a brother... But then to be honest she'd hardly spoken to Ann in the past week. The young couple had picked her up at the airport, driven her to her own flat in Islington, north London, dropped the bombshell of their engagement, told her to attend this celebration dinner at the weekend and then they'd taken off the next day. The two telephone conversations Rose had had with her Aunt Jean in Richmond, had been about the arrangements for the party, and if the truth be known, Rose had slept for much of the past week.

Glancing around the comfortable bedroom, Rose was tempted to drop down on the queen-sized bed and sleep again. But mindful of Teresa's instruction to come down for cocktails at seven, she unpacked her weekend case instead, placing her underwear in the top drawer of a lovely old pine chest, and the rest of her clothes in the matching wardrobe. Rose glanced around the room. It really was lovely; the pine furniture was genuinely old, and the sprigged wallpaper and matching drapes and duvet, were charming. She investigated a door to one side and found a neat little shower room with vanity basin and toilet.

Stripping off her clothes, she stepped into the shower stall and turned on the taps. The warm spray caressed her body and she sighed with relief. When she'd arrived back in England last week, Ann had informed her almost straight away that she was engaged. Rose had wondered if her cousin was too young at twenty-one. Plus she'd felt guilty because Rose had been indirectly responsible for the couple meeting. She'd rented out her apartment in London to students for the past three years, allowing Ann to stay rent free. Jamie and another student, Mike, had shared the three-bedroomed flat with Ann. Jamie and Ann had been drawn together when they realised they only lived a few miles apart in Yorkshire.

Everything was going to be fine, Rose told herself as the hot jets of water eased the tension from her taut muscles and relaxed her mind.

Twenty minutes later, Rose closed the bedroom door behind her, and hurried along down the stairs. The sitting room door was slightly ajar and she could hear the sound of chatter and laughter. Drawing a deep breath she pushed open the door and entered.

'Last as usual, Rosalyn! But you look as lovely as ever.' Her Uncle Alex was standing by the fireplace, a smile on his face, and Rose started to cross the room towards him. But then it happened...

Teresa moved from the entrance to the conservatory. 'You know everyone Rosalyn, except my brother. Please, allow me to introduce you to Xavier.'

At the sound of the man's name Rose's step faltered. It could not be! Such an outrageous coincidence just wasn't possible. Nervously she smoothed her damp palms down over her slim hips and almost in slow motion she turned towards Teresa, and the man beside her exiting the conservatory beside the hostess. Fate could not be so cruel, she told herself, but with a terrible sense of inevitability about it, she slowly tilted back her head to look up at the man.

'My brother Xavier Valdespino, and this is Ann's cousin, Dr. Rosalyn May.'

She barely heard the introduction but she did not need to...

Xavier Valdespino gazed down at her, his dark face

shadowed by the evening sunlight shining through the conservatory behind him. He stepped forward, his bronzed features set in a mask of social politeness.

'It is a pleasure to meet you. Dr....' His deep voice hesitated a moment. 'Rosalyn May.'

He reached out and took her hand in his. Numb with shock Rose let him and felt the strength of his long fingers close around hers. Panic flared briefly in her wide green eyes as they met his but his golden-brown eyes smiled coolly down at her without the slightest hint of recognition in his gaze.

'How do you do,' she murmured politely. But her heart was pounding like jungle drums in her chest. Seeing him again after a decade was an experience that needed all her self-control. His tall, broad-shouldered presence exuded the same aura of vibrant masculinity which she'd recognised and succumbed to at their first meeting. Only years of discipline in controlling her emotions enabled her to behave with the modicum of social necessity.

'Better for having met you.' And, before Rose realised what he intended, his head bowed and he raised her hand to plant firm warm lips on the back of her hand. In any other man it would have been over the top but somehow from this man it seemed perfectly natural.

Electric sensation sizzled through her flesh and she tugged her hand away, her mouth opening and closing without a sound.

'And may I say; I concur completely with your Uncle, you do look lovely.' Dark eyes swept down from the flame of her hair, and lingered on her face then her green silk dress and finally on the long length of her legs, before returning to her face.

She felt the colour rise in her cheeks, and with it her temper. Her thick-lashed green eyes swept over his tall frame with the same studied intensity. He was powerfully built with not an ounce of superfluous flesh on the long lean length of his body. Clothed in an immaculately tailored black dinner suit, with a white silk dress shirt, and black bow tie, he looked exactly what he was: a hugely successful business tycoon, who financed his own formula-one racing team as a hobby. Now he was acting like the womanizer she knew he was, never mind the fact he was married!

'Thank you,' she said calmly recovering from the horrendous shock of being presented to a man she had not seen for ten years and had hoped never to see again in this lifetime.

Then she noticed what shock had made her miss at first glance. The incredibly handsome face was not quite as she remembered. A deep scar curved in a sickle shape from his ear to his jaw on one side of his face, marring the perfect olive-skinned complexion. Her professional interest aroused, she realised he'd obviously had a skin graft sometime ago, possibly for a burn, as the skin encircled by the scar was paler and continued down beneath the collar of his shirt.

'I believe I am to be your partner for the evening, Rosalyn. I may call you Rosalyn?' One superbly arched dark brow lifted in query. 'Unless you prefer another name?' he prompted smoothly.

'Another name! Well, most people call me Rose, apart from my Aunt and Uncle, but I have no preference,' Rose answered cagily, her green eyes narrowing on his hard unyielding face. Had he recognised her after all? She couldn't be sure, she'd been a teenager when they'd met; she'd been much slimmer with short straight hair a couple of shades darker than it was now; the African sun over the past three years had lightened it quite a lot. Whereas he'd been already a mature man of twenty-nine and the intervening years had hardly changed him at all, except for the scar.

'With your permission I will call you Rosalyn. It's such a very feminine name—it suits you,' his deep voice opined throatily.

He'd lost none of his charm, that was for sure, Rose acknowledged. Thankfully he did not seem to know who she was. Then why would he? As far as he was concerned she'd been little more than a one-night stand, one among thousands. She was flattering herself to imagine he would remember her, let alone the name she'd used for the brief time she'd been a model.

'Whatever you prefer,' Rose said casually, all too aware of his intense male scrutiny. His dark eyes roamed over her body, lingering on her physical attributes in turn. She felt as though he had mentally stripped her naked, but she was almost sure it was not memory prompting his interest but simply a purely male reaction to a halfway attractive woman.

'Now Uncle Xavier, no hogging my soon-to-be-cousin; the poor girl might die of thirst!' Jamie appeared suddenly at her side holding out a crystal flute filled to the brim with sparkling Dom Perignon. 'Champagne, Rose?'

Glad of the interruption, Rose turned slightly and took the proffered glass with a smile.

'A toast,' Jamie offered with a broad grin, and glancing around the room he lifted his glass. 'To Ann and I, as nobody else seems to be going to do it.'

In the congratulations and laughter that followed, Rose took the opportunity to slip across the room to her Aunt Jean, but she had the uncanny feeling that a pair of dark assessing eyes were following her every move. Maybe she should have admitted to him that they'd met before, and they could have talked as old friends. No—they had never been friends. But lovers, yes!

The memory made her wince. Pain like a red-hot needle pierced her heart for a second, and she couldn't stop herself glancing back at the man who'd caused it. The softly curling raven hair was longer now, with silver wings curving around his ears. The fine lines around his eyes, and the deep grooves on either side of his sinfully sexy mouth were deeper, but he was still the most staggeringly attractive man she'd ever seen. A pity his nature was anything but attractive... At that moment his dark head lifted from a conversation with his brother-in-law, and his piercing eyes clashed with hers. She watched as he moved towards her. A bit like a rabbit caught in the headlights of a car, she was helpless to look away. What on earth was happening to her? She was long past this kind of nonsense. But to her chagrin when he reached her, he glanced past her to say something to her Aunt and Uncle.

'Alex, Jean, David informs me the taxis have arrived so if you are ready we can leave.' Only then did he look at Rose. 'Us four are to share one car, Rosalyn, if that's all right with you?'

'Yes, of course.' What else could she say?

'You're sure? he asked with slow deliberation. 'I got the distinct impression you couldn't get away from me fast enough,' he drawled mockingly, his eyes still holding hers. 'I hope I was wrong.'

Rose could feel the angry colour rising in her cheeks, but she swallowed down a scathing retort and got slowly to her feet. 'You were,' she replied lightly. 'Shall we go? I'm starving.'

Once again, more blatantly this time, his gaze ran the length of her shapely body, and then rested on the classic oval of her face. 'I know the feeling.' Curving a large hand around her elbow he added, 'My hunger is rising by the minute.'

She cast him a swift wary glance beneath the thick veil of her lashes. She knew by the suggestive tone of his voice that he was being deliberately provocative. The very last thing she wanted was to spend an evening in Xavier's company, and she almost groaned out loud when she realised, never mind the evening, it was perfectly possible she would have to spend all weekend with him. She was not due to depart until Monday morning with her Aunt and Uncle, as she was going to stay with them for a week or two. Her other suitcase was still in her car along with a pile of books she had been promising herself to read for years.

'When are you returning to Spain?' she blurted without thinking as he led her out of the house and to the waiting limousine. The warmth of his hand on her bare arm reminding her of feelings she'd thought were long forgotten.

'You're not very flattering to a man's ego, Rosalyn. We've only just met and you seem to have a great desire to see me depart,' he drawled and she could see the mockery in his dark eyes as he met her gaze.

'No, really, I was only making polite conversation,' she denied flatly.

'Forgive me, I am not well versed on the social niceties of the English.' His dark head bent and he murmured in her ear, 'Perhaps you can teach me.' He promptly released her, and stood back to allow her Aunt and Uncle to get in the car first.

Thank heaven the journey to the hotel was only ten minutes Rose thought angrily. She cast a sideways glance at the man seated beside her. He was talking quite easily to her Aunt and Uncle, while she was tense with the effort to hold herself away from the long body so close to her own. His shoulder and thigh lightly brushed hers every so often as the chauffeur negotiated the twists and turns of the narrow Yorkshire lanes. But Xavier was obviously not concerned by the physical contact—instead his expression remained coolly aloof.

'Rosalyn was in Spain once.' Aunt Jean's comment impinged on Rose's distracted thoughts.

'On holiday,' Rose cut in quickly. No way did she want her aunt mentioning she'd once been a model. It might just jog the arrogant devil's memory.

'So you've visited my country, Rosalyn? Where did you stay?' She could see no hint of anything but polite query in the expression that met hers, and she chastised herself for overreacting. The man did not know her from Adam.

'Oh I stayed in Barcelona; a wonderful city,' she responded coolly.

'I agree with you. I used to visit Barcelona every year for the Grand Prix racing. But I have not been for some years.'

Rose gave him a considering look. Except for a slight narrowing of his heavy-lidded dark eyes, his expression remained one of polite interest, but for a second she wondered if it was overly polite—as though he was concealing something. She sure as hell would not want to play poker with the man, she thought dryly.

'You used to race cars?' Alex cut in enthusiastically.

'No. I used to support a team, as a hobby.' Xavier aimed his response at Alex. 'But unfortunately other commitments took over and I no longer have the time. But I still love cars and have quite a collection at home.'

'Have you seen Rosalyn's car? It's a beauty.'

Xavier turned back to Rose. 'Yes, I saw it in the drive—an E-type Jaguar.' His dark eyes caught and held hers. 'Rather a fast car for a lady, I would have thought.'

'Rather a chauvinistic statement for the twenty-first century, I would have thought,' Rose shot back with feeling. Male chauvinism of any kind was absolute anathema to her.

'You are not one of those rampant feminists who believe a man is only good for one thing, are you?'

There was no mistaking the cynical amusement in his tone. 'And if I am?' she asked curtly.

'It has always been my opinion that beautiful women should be protected, pampered and adored by the male of the species, after all it was what they were put on earth for, that and having babies,' he replied with slow deliberation. 'It is such a waste when a woman looks like an angel but has the mind of a steel trap.' His hand lifted and casually caught a single wayward curl of red hair and tucked it behind her ear. 'A loose strand.'

Loose strand be blowed! Rose's green eyes blazed with outrage, angry colour rising in her face. He was deliberately winding her up and she could sense the amusement lurking beneath his cool gaze. 'Better than no mind at all, like some men I have met,' she returned furiously, oddly disturbed by the touch of his long finger on her cheek.

'It was meant as a joke,' Xavier said dryly. 'And perhaps I thought it would be amusing to discover if you had a temper to match your hair.'

# CHAPTER TWO

ROSE GLARED at Xavier, and jerked her head back. 'If you'd spent the last few years in the trouble spots of the world, like I've been, most recently Africa, and had to repair the damage done to young girls by a male chauvinistic society, you would not find the subject so amusing. Girls with their bodies mangled by a badly done circumcision, simply because it is the custom. Or had to watch a fourteen-year-old die in childbirth having been repeatedly raped until she was pregnant and then married off to her rapist. Officially against the law, but a male tradition and so the law turns a blind eye. People like you disgust me,' she declared emphatically.

Xavier, his mouth twisting wryly at the way Rose was looking at him said quietly, 'I seem to have upset you, and that was not my intention. I apologise most sincerely.'

Alex intervened, 'I shouldn't worry about it, Xavier. She has a quick temper. It was your bad luck you touched on a subject that is a particular hobby-horse of hers. She'll get over it.'

'Do you mind, Uncle? I can speak for myself,' Rose cut in, ignoring Xavier's apology. She hated injustice of any kind but particularly against children. And deep down she realised the way Xavier had behaved towards her when she'd been barely nineteen and little more than a child herself still made her burn with rage and resentment. She'd thought she'd put the past behind her, but seeing Xavier again had brought back a lot of bitter memories. And he, damn him, did not even recognise her!

The hotel they were going to for dinner was one Rose knew well. As a child she'd spent most of her school holidays with her Aunt and Uncle in the Yorkshire town of Richmond, and dined at the place frequently.

Teresa sat at one end of the rectangular table, while her husband David sat at the other end. Seeing her Aunt Jean and Uncle Alex sit down, Rose hastily grabbed the seat next to them. No way did she want to end up next to Xavier. She picked up the linen napkin provided, and spread it on her lap heaving a silent sigh of relief. But her relief was short-lived when she looked up and discovered her nemesis was sitting directly opposite her with Ann then Jamie next to him.

Her startled gaze collided with Xavier's and for a second Rose imagined she saw something dark and sinister flicker in the depths of his eyes. Quickly she hid behind the menu the waiter had handed her. But she couldn't concentrate on the list of dishes on offer. Instead she was intensely aware of the hard cynical man sitting opposite to her. A dozen questions spun around in her mind. What joke of fate had led Ann to meet his nephew Jamie—in Rose's own flat for heaven's sake? And why was Xavier here alone? She knew for an absolute fact he was married, so where was his wife? Did he have children? she wondered. The thought made her heart miss a beat.

She glanced sideways at her uncle. Her aunt and uncle and Ann were her only family since the death of her parents in a plane crash when she was seventeen. And once Ann was married to Jamie where did that leave her? She could not contemplate a life that included Xavier as part of her family. Weddings, birthdays, christenings with the arrogant Xavier Valdespino in attendance, her mind boggled at the thought. She would never be able to keep up the pretence of not knowing him. In fact she'd severe doubts as to whether she would be able to last the weekend, without telling the man exactly what she thought of him. He was a callous, rotten, devious, chauvinistic pig of a man, and she hated him with a depth of passion that was alien to her usual caring nature. She wasn't proud of it, but she couldn't help it.

'Have you decided what you want to eat, Rosalyn?' His deep melodious voice drawling her full name cut into her musings. 'Or shall I choose for you?'

His audacity at suggesting he should order for her grated on her over-sensitive nerves and lowering the menu, her stormy eyes scanned his ruggedly handsome face. On any other man the scar would have appeared ugly but on Xavier it gave him a rakish piratical air, and highlighted the perfection of his bone structure. She knew he was deliberately baiting her with his offer to choose.

She dropped the menu on the table. 'I don't need your help. I will have the melon followed by a prawn salad.'

'Watching your figure?' one dark brow arched quizzically. 'There's really no need—you're quite exquisitely proportioned already. As I am sure many men must have told you before me,' he opined smoothly.

He'd lost none of his legendary charm; the gleam of appreciation in his dark eyes was precise enough to show interest, but not enough to offend. Oh, he was good! Rose thought, but two could play at that game.

'You flatter me, Señor Valdespino,' she said coyly fluttering her eyelashes at him.

His mouth twisted. 'Xavier, please. And I do not flatter. You are a beautiful woman in every way,' he added after a deliberate pause, subjecting her to a more detailed scrutiny, his eyes lingering on the curve of her breasts exposed by the neckline of her dress, then ever so slowly back to her face. 'Perfection that it would be a crime to spoil by a foolish desire to slim.'

His crack about dieting was frighteningly familiar. He'd said the same thing the night they'd spent together. Rose's green eyes narrowed warily on his tanned face, but his expression gave nothing away, and forcing herself to meet his cynical gaze she responded, 'Oh, I never slim, I simply fancy the salad, and I bet you're going to order the steak?' Widening her eyes to their fullest extent she added in mock surprise, 'Oh! Maybe not, I forgot you are all bull.' She wanted to add a four-letter word beginning with 'S,' but bit her tongue in time.

'Rosalyn,' Aunt Jean admonished. 'What a thing to say.'

Completely absorbed in her exchange with Xavier, Rose hadn't realised everyone else had stopped talking. But the laughter in Ann's and Jamie's eyes, told her they'd heard.

'What?' Rose queried with a swift glance around the table at her companions. Casually shrugging her shoulders, she continued, 'I simply meant that Xavier is Spanish. As I understand it, they eat a lot of bull meat in Spain, what with all the bullfights they have.' She played the innocent for all she was worth. And was relieved to see her Aunt and Uncle bought it, but one glance at Xavier's face told her he was not fooled. A hard smile twisted his sensuous lips; he knew she'd intended to insult him.

'Such an instant rapport between two virtual strangers is truly amazing. You read my mind, Rosalyn.' There was a faint hint of cynicism to the words Rose could not fail to recognise.

'I will have the smoked salmon starter, and I *am* going to have the steak, and I really do not mind if it is your cow meat, even though the rest of Europe saw fit to ban it for some considerable time. I am sure it will be just as tasty as Spanish bull.'

Sarcastic devil... But she was saved from having to respond by the waiter arriving to take their order.

Champagne was delivered to the table, and the meal took on a festive glow as David toasted the happy couple, and everyone joined in. The first course arrived and Rose resolved to keep her head down and only speak when spoken to, but it was not that simple.

Jamie, high on love and maybe a little too much champagne, insisted on drinking a toast to everyone—including Rose. 'If it hadn't been for you letting out your London home I may never have met Ann.'

'I only hope you don't live to regret it,' Rose said with a grin. 'I know my cousin of old; she can be quite a handful! I remember the time when she was ten and she talked me into following the local hunt on a couple of donkeys Uncle Alex kept at the time. I wouldn't care but I was nearly eighteen and not even in favour of blood sports!'

'Now that I would have liked to see.' Xavier leaned forward slightly, pushing his empty plate to one side, his face on a level with Rose's. 'Do you enjoy riding, Rosalyn?' he asked with a bland smile.

Boldly she held his gaze, and she knew his question had nothing to do with blood sports. The golden gleam of a primitive predatory male sparkled in his eyes, the black pupils dilated ever so slightly. But she also sensed beneath the surface charm of his smile a supreme arrogance that was distinctly threatening. This man was used to getting any woman he wanted with out expending too much effort at all.

'I used to when I visited my Aunt and Uncle,' she confirmed lightly, ignoring the challenge in his eyes and answering him factually. 'But for the past few years I've not really had the opportunity. Unless of course you consider sitting on a camel in the Kalahari Desert, but I doubt very much if that would appeal to a man of your—sophisticated status.'

'I could be tempted if you were to accompany me,' Xavier responded his voice deepening seductively. 'A beautiful woman is a great incentive to perform well.'

Rose eyed him quizzically; there was something not quite right. Even when he was flirting with her, there was a certain aloofness about him that was at odds with the compliments he was handing out. But she wasn't about to waste her time analysing the man. She wanted nothing to do with him.

'You're wasting your time, Señor Valdespino.'

'Oh, I don't think so. After all, the night is still young.' He leaned back in his chair and indicated to the wine waiter, and ordered more champagne. Then glancing back at her he added, 'A few more bottles of champagne and who knows what might happen, Rosalyn, darling.' He'd drawled the endearment teasingly.

The whole company greeted his comment with genuine laughter, and he grinned, his lips curling back over brilliant white teeth. But only Rose noticed the smile didn't reach his eyes.

'I doubt if your wife would find your comment so amusing,' she snapped back.

'And what makes you think I have a wife?' Xavier queried silkily, and raising his glass to his lips he took a long drink before returning the glass to the table. Leaning back in his seat he observed her beneath hooded eyelids.

Rose was all too aware of the sudden silence that had greeted her statement and the sudden tension in the man opposite. She realised she'd almost revealed she knew him, or at least knew a lot about him. Thinking quickly she tried to hide her blunder by blaming his earlier chauvinistic attitude.

'Well a man of your age with your views…' One delicate eyebrow arched cynically. 'I took it for granted you would be married with three or four children at your feet and probably a pregnant wife at home.'

'Your perception is really quite remarkable. One would almost think we had met before.'

Rose stiffened. He had recognised her! But he continued, his voice as unyielding as his expression. 'Yes, I have been married, but no children I'm afraid, and my wife died two years ago.'

'I am sorry,' she mumbled, her face going scarlet. Rose wanted the ground to open and swallow her. Her dislike for the man had led her into being deliberately rude. But Ann jumping to her feet saved her from any further embarrassment.

'Excuse me, but I must visit the rest room,' Ann said quite loudly. 'Come with me, Rose.'

Rose grasped the chance to escape and pushing back her chair she walked around the table and out of the dining room with her cousin.

'My God, Rose, what are you trying to do?' Ann said urgently, dragging her by the arm across the elegant lobby and into the powder room. 'End my engagement before it has begun?'

'I don't know what you mean,' Rose dismissed, glancing around the mirrored walls and finally down at Ann, immediately perturbed by the agitation in her pretty face.

'Oh! For heaven's sake, Rose! Xavier Valdespino is to all intents and purposes the head of the family. His father Don Pablo Ortega Valdespino is retired and very ill. So if Xavier decided against my marrying Jamie, that's it… I know Jamie loves me, but it is his uncle who pays his allowance and his college fees and he still has a year to do. This dinner was supposed to unite our two families, and you've done nothing but insult Xavier since you met him. What is the matter with you? He's a charming, polite man. A bit old, but not bad-looking if you discount the scar. Is that it, his scar?' Ann's puzzled brown eyes fixed on her cousin. 'You're a doctor! I can't believe you would let a thing like that influence your opinion of him.'

'No, no, of course not,' Rose denied adamantly, mortified that Ann should even think such a thing. 'But I never realised how important it was to you and Jamie that his uncle approved. David and Teresa must be quite wealthy in their own right, surely? The farm is vast and then there are the racing stables. Don't you think you're putting too much importance on the opinion of an Uncle?' she queried bluntly.

Ann grimaced, 'It is obvious you've been far too long abroad, and too involved in your career; you don't realise what is happening in the rest of the world. For the past few years British farmers have been going out of business by the dozen. Mad Cow Disease and the European ban on beef exports have finished off hundreds. The racing stables pay their way but only just, according to Jamie. If it weren't for his uncle's help the farm would have gone to the wall. So for heaven's sake try and be nice to Xavier or you will wreck everything. We are counting on him giving us the money for Jamie to set up in his own practice as a Vet in two or three years' time.'

'I never realised,' Rose said slowly, frowning at her cousin. She'd lost touch with Ann over the years she realised guiltily. The young girl who'd followed her around as a child had grown up into a confident young woman who knew exactly what she wanted from life. Rose sighed. 'You're right, I have probably been away too long. I have forgotten how to behave.' She excused her behaviour. 'But from now on I will be sweetness and light with Señor

Xavier Valdespino, I promise.' She glanced at her reflection in the mirrored wall, smoothed a few errant curls back from her brow, and straightened her shoulders. 'He will have no reason to complain I assure you, Ann.'

'That's more like it,' Ann grinned and glanced appreciatively at the reflection of the tall elegant woman beside her. 'The supermodel is back.'

'Don't mention I was a model,' Rose returned quickly.

'Why ever not? You will have him eating out of your hand. I can see he fancies you.'

'No,' she protested. 'I mean it, Ann. Not one word about modelling.'

'Okay,' Ann said easily. 'But you have to keep your side of the bargain; no more snide remarks. Be nice to the man.' Her cousin chuckled softly. 'And hey, even a dedicated career girl like you must see he is quite a catch. A bit of a cold fish admittedly, but wealthy, sophisticated and single, what more could you want?'

A *cold fish* was going a bit far but Rose knew what Ann meant. Xavier had the poised and watchful air of a man who was in the family scene, but yet not quite part of it. Detached, somehow above it. As for the rest at one time Rose inwardly acknowledged she would have agreed with Ann, but not anymore. 'You know, cousin mine,' she said slipping her arm through Ann's and walking back towards the dining room. 'I have just realised you have quite a mercenary little streak in your otherwise perfect nature.'

'No. But I love Jamie with all my heart, and I am simply being practical.'

There was no answer to that and Rose did not attempt to make one.

'We were beginning to wonder if you'd got lost,' Jamie said as the two women returned to their places at the table.

'Your youth is showing, Jamie,' Xavier remarked. 'We

older men know from experience,' he exchanged looks with
Alex and David, 'Ladies always go to the rest room in twos
as if it were an annexe to Noah's Ark, and when they get
there, they have a good gossip, and pick the men in their
lives to bits while us poor men are left waiting for hours.'

His comment was greeted by laughter and the conversation became general.

Rose ate the food put in front of her without really tasting
it, and tried her damnedest not to look at Xavier, but for
some reason her eyes were constantly drawn to his hard
face. He was a brilliant conversationalist, and the topics
discussed ranged from the state of the stock market to the
state of David's racehorses. The main course was cleared
away and the dessert ordered and eaten when the conversation got around to the next race meeting at York the following weekend, and somehow then on to travel.

'Your Aunt tells me you have been abroad for three
years,' Xavier said, the first direct comment he had made
to Rose in over an hour. 'You must have had some interesting experiences.'

Mindful of her promise to Ann, Rose forced herself to
smile. 'A few, but mostly it was work and more work.
There is a dreadful shortage of doctors in almost all the
African states, especially in the rural areas. People in the
west are so used to simply making a phone call and an
ambulance arriving, we forget a lot of the world is not so
fortunate.' Warming to her subject her face glowed with an
inner fervour, that fascinated the man watching her, something she was totally unaware of.

Jean cut into the conversation. 'Really Rose, do you have
to?'

'But it is shaming to all of us, Aunt Jean,' her green eyes
flashed at her aunt. 'That in the twenty-first century there
are still many places in the world where a woman will walk

for days with a sick child simply to get to a clinic, never mind a hospital.'

'Rose. Not tonight, you know what your superior said: three months rest and relaxation,' her aunt reminded her.

'That does not prevent me from having an opinion,' she began to argue, and stopped abruptly, at the sight of Ann's frowning face across the table.

'You're on an extended holiday,' Xavier prompted filling the sudden pause in the conversation. His dark eyes narrowed intently on her beautiful face. 'I did not realise.'

'No reason why you should.' Rose lifted her eyes to his, and took a swift involuntary breath. Something flickered in the brilliant gaze something dark and vaguely dangerous. 'After all we've only just met,' she lied.

Quite unbidden into her mind sprang the sudden erotic image of his tall, powerful bronzed body, totally naked, sprawled on black satin sheets, and her stomach clenched in fierce sexual response. Her reaction stunned her. She'd tried sex once again two years ago, and decided it was definitely overrated and had not had a vaguely sensual experience since, so why now? Perhaps because her anger at Xavier Valdespino was tempered by pity for the man on hearing his wife had died. Suddenly she was seeing him simply as a very virile man.

She tore her gaze away from his, her eyes dropping to his strong jaw, the vicious scar and the hint of hardness in his chiselled mouth. But that was a mistake. Involuntarily, her tongue slipped out between her teeth and licked her bottom lip as if the taste of him still lingered a decade later. She swallowed hard. Oh, be sensible, she told herself, and for a second she closed her eyes, to dispel the haunting images of the past. When she opened them again. It took her a moment to realise Xavier was still talking to her.

'You must come with Ann and Jamie tomorrow, I insist.'

Rose shook her head in confusion, her green gaze fixing warily on the man opposite. What was he talking about? Go where with Jamie and Ann?

'That is a great idea,' Ann joined the conversation. 'I was thinking I would be outnumbered by men and with no one to shop with.'

'You must come, Rose, anything to save me from shopping,' Jamie laughingly agreed.

'Yes, it will do you the world of good.' Aunt Jean was all for it.

But *what?* Bemused, Rose glanced around the smiling faces; everyone seemed to be in favour of her going out with Jamie and Ann tomorrow. Maybe a day in Harrogate or Leeds, shopping…? She looked at Ann's smiling face, the anticipation in her brown eyes, and mindful of her promise to her cousin. She said, 'Yes, okay, where exactly is it that we are going?'

'To my home in Spain,' Xavier offered smoothly. Rising to his feet he pushed back his chair. 'And now we have that settled, I believe the coffee is served in the lounge. And no doubt these two youngsters want to get down to the disco and meet their friends.'

'Wait a minute I can't go to Spain!' Rose jumped to her feet. 'I thought you meant a day in Leeds to shop, or something.' She was babbling, she knew. What had she agreed to? In the general exodus she glanced frantically around, and they all stopped. Suddenly seven pairs of eyes were fixed on her with varying degrees of amusement.

'Of course you can,' Aunt Jean said. 'It will be much more fun for you than staying with Alex and I. Do you have your passport with you?'

'Yes, but…'

'Good, then it's no problem,' Jean stated emphatically.

'But I can't just swan off to Spain, I mean.' Rose cast a

swift glance at Xavier, but there was no help there. His dark eyes gleamed with devilish amusement as he watched her dig herself deeper. 'Well, your grandfather is ill, Jamie,' she appealed to the younger man. 'He won't want to entertain a stranger in his house.'

'Actually the opposite is true,' Teresa said firmly. 'My father is of the old school; very traditional. To be honest he was not very happy about Ann staying at the hacienda on her own with Jamie before they are married without a chaperone present.'

'A chaperone!' Rose repeated incredulously. Was the man still living in the Dark Ages or what? 'You must be joking!' But no one was laughing...

'My sister is correct,' Xavier drawled, his cool gaze captured and held her flashing green eyes, as he calmly responded, 'It is our custom for an older female relative to act as a chaperone for the young bride-to-be. You would be doing Teresa and I a great favour and giving our father peace of mind while he is so ill.'

'Xavier is right,' Ann said moving to stand beside Rose and laying a hand on her arm. 'Please say you will come; I don't want to upset Jamie's grandfather before I am even married.'

Rose's mouth worked but no sound came out. Her furious expression narrowed on Xavier's bland face. The swine was enjoying this, and she felt like some aging spinster maiden aunt. She looked back down at Ann, and saw the worry behind her brown eyes.

'Yes. Okay,' she capitulated, she could not do much else. But how on earth she was going to put up with living in the same house as Xavier Valdespino she had no idea.

'Great. See you downstairs, later,' Ann gave her a hug. 'It will be fun to have you with us in Spain.' And with a wink she walked off.

'Allow me to escort you to the lounge,' Xavier offered with a hand in the small of her back. 'You look rather dazed. Too much champagne, perhaps?'

He was laughing at her; she could hear it in his voice. The arrogant devil knew damn well that she did not want to go to Spain. How in heaven's name had she landed herself in such a mess?

'Put like that how can I refuse?' Rose replied dryly. But with his large hand spread across the small of her back, the warmth of his touch sending quivers of awareness down her spine, it took every speck of willpower she possessed to control. She knew in the interest of self-preservation she should have refused. His intimidating height, and powerful body so close to her own set every one of her senses on full alert as they crossed into the lounge.

It was with an inward sigh of relief that she felt his hand fall from her back. Rose glanced at the three sofas arranged around a low coffee table and moved to join her Uncle Alex on one of them, smoothing the soft fabric of her dress down over her hips with palms that were slightly damp. Xavier chose to sit opposite with his sister, and Aunt Jean and David occupied the third sofa. Coffee was served, and the conversation revolved around the Spanish home of the Valdespino's. Apparently the ranch was some miles from Seville, in the high plains of the interior, but the family kept a town house in Seville as well.

'I can promise you will not be bored,' Xavier said serenely, his dark eyes lazily roaming over her beautiful face. 'My father is at present in the town house, mainly so he can be near the hospital if the need arises while I am not there. Hopefully you and Ann will have the opportunity to see a little of the city, and then depending on what my father's doctor thinks, we will all go back to the ranch.'

'It sounds very nice,' Rose said agreeably, just managing

to keep a note of mockery from her voice. Who was she kidding; the thought of spending a week in his company sounded like the holiday from hell! What was more, she was sure he knew exactly how she felt! For the past half hour she'd watched him perform. The suave sophisticated business man had led the conversation skilfully. Never once paying more attention to Rose than he did to her Aunt or his sister. But there was something... Beneath his cool, confident surface she caught glimpses of something primitive, a gleam in his dark eyes when they deigned to rest on her that was anything but cool.

Maybe she was being paranoid, transferring her own banked-down anger onto him. Shaking her head she got to her feet as the receptionist arrived to inform them the cars were waiting.

For a few moments Teresa was deep in conversation with Xavier in their native language. Rose took the opportunity to move to her Aunt Jean and murmur, 'Not the ordeal you imagined, I think it all went off very well.'

'Exceptionally well,' a deep husky voice cut in.

Rose spun around to find Xavier standing so close he was invading her personal space and instinctively she splayed her hand across his chest in self-defence. 'I didn't see you.' She could feel the heat of his body, the steady beat of his heart through the fine silk of his shirt and she pulled her hand back, her fingers burning as though she had touched hot coals. 'You shouldn't creep up on people like that.'

'"Creep up,"' he parroted, mockery gleaming in the depths of his eyes. 'No one has ever accused me of being a creep before. I think your superior is quite right, you are far too nervous, you do need a change.'

'Exactly,' Aunt Jean agreed. 'Now you run along with Xavier to the disco, and let your hair down, you have been far too serious for far too long, Rosalyn. But you will check on Ann and Jamie for us won't you?'

Which was why ten minutes later Rose found herself at the entrance to a noisy basement club with strobelights flashing and a strong male hand pressing at the base of her spine urging her forward.

'You can't possibly want to stay here.' Glancing up at her companion and catching a glimpse of such icy derision in his black eyes she instinctively recoiled from his guiding hand.

'Sorry, I can't hear you.' Without warning he reached out and pulled her into his arms, his dark head bent towards her and his mouth moved against the soft curve of her ear. 'I gather you are past such simple amusement, Rosalyn. But one dance, a swift check on the youngsters and our duty to their parents will be achieved and we can leave. Agreed?'

With the warmth of his breath in her ear her heart jumped and breathlessly she mouthed her agreement. It was her bad luck the DJ chose that moment to play a ballad. Xavier held her fast with one strong hand between her shoulder blades the other encircling her tiny waist to settle low on her hip. Too low for decency, Rose thought. But it got worse; with her breasts flattened against his broad chest, he moved her to the rhythm of the music with an underlying sensuality that aroused a swift pang of response she tried her utmost to ignore.

Her tension ratio shot up to astronomical heights. Every cell in her body clamouring to surrender to the magnetic pull of his devastatingly powerful masculinity. She should get away now, common sense told her. Xavier Valdespino was a very dangerous man. But contrarily she was offended at the implication she was too old to enjoy a disco.

So when the music changed, and with his black eyes

dancing, he said huskily, 'Can you Salsa?' Stupidly she said 'yes'...

He should have looked foolish; he was much older than any other male in the room. Instead he looked like every woman's fantasy.

'Way to go, uncle!' Jamie's voice echoed above the music, and Rose glanced briefly at the young couple that had appeared next to them on the dance floor.

But her eyes were quickly drawn back to the man holding her. Xavier's large body moved with a sinuous grace, and a sensual awareness that was as erotic as it was arousing. Cynically, Rose recognised it was the dichotomy between the aloof, strong-willed powerful male, and the red-hot sexuality he exuded without even trying that made every woman in the place cast him blatant sideways glances.

Whether it was the champagne she had drunk or simply the angry frustration that had simmered inside her since meeting the man, Rose did not know, but the brush of his long body against her own was a tantalising challenge she could not resist and she threw herself uninhibitedly into the dance.

When the music ended, he hauled her close against the hard heat of his body and she was lost. She felt the hard pressure of his arousal against her belly, and knew then that he was equally affected, she watched as his dark head lowered towards her. He was going to kiss her. Her lips parted invitingly. But abruptly he straightened up his strong hands curved around her shoulders and casually he stepped back. His dark eyes sweeping down over her from head to toe, his expression coldly remote...

# CHAPTER THREE

CONFUSED, Rose stared dazedly up at his face. A ray of strobe lighting illuminated his features, and for an instant he looked like the devil himself.

'Thank you. You dance well,' he said with practised politeness, his hands dropping from her shoulders.

'Thank you,' she mumbled, her face burning with embarrassment. What was happening to her? How could she have been so stupid as to think a man like Xavier Valdespino was going to kiss her in the middle of a crowded dance floor? Had she taken leave of her senses or what? Averting her face she took a step backwards. 'So do you,' she tagged on, because it was all she could think of, and, face it, she told herself, it was the truth. The man had all the moves and a body to die for, and she should know...

'Come, I think we have done our duty. The young couple are well able to take care of themselves and I need a long cool drink.' Taking her arm he led her towards the exit and back upstairs, to the relative quiet of the cocktail lounge. It said something about Rose's confused emotions that she let him.

He ordered two lemonades from a passing waiter, and then urged Rose to sit down on a long sofa. 'Too much champagne and dancing we are liable to dehydrate,' he commented blandly lowering his long body down beside her.

She turned her head slightly forcing herself to meet his dark eyes. 'I do know that. I am a doctor,' she said, irked by the fact that she was hot, her hair escaping from its

38

former neat style into curling disarray, while Xavier looked remarkably cool and in control. Even his damned bow tie had not moved, she thought bitterly.

The waiter arrived with their drinks and Rose hastily grabbed the glass and drained it in a second. Her companion did the same.

'I needed that,' she admitted placing the glass back on the table.

'*Sí,*' Xavier agreed after he finished his, lounging back against the arm of the sofa. A respectable space between them, he studied her from beneath hooded lids.

'A very English Doctor who dances like a Latin!' His dark brows rose in mock astonishment and he smiled. 'Tell me your secret? Where did you learn to Salsa?'

It was an innocuous question, and Rose grasped the chance to indulge in a normal conversation. Hoping it would diffuse the sexual tension that had consumed her for the past hour, though seeing Xavier's interested but arrogantly aloof expression told her he had suffered from no such affliction.

'In Africa,' she said honestly and paused for a moment, happy memories making her green eyes sparkle with reminiscent humour.

'And,' he prompted.

'Dominic, an archaeologist from Buenos Aries ended up at our hospital in Somalia. Apparently he'd been travelling privately when he was robbed and was lucky to escape with his life. No money, no clothes, a black eye and a cracked skull, but bizarrely he'd managed to hang on to a CD of Salsa music. He played the CD night and day on the music centre at the residence. By the time he left three months later I could dance the Salsa, the Tango and the Samba. He was a very good singer as well,' Rose offered with a smile. The lemonade had cooled her down, and the night was almost over—Xavier had ordered the car along with the drinks. She could afford to be friendly and let her guard down.

She'd no idea how tempting she looked to the man watching her. His dark profile clenched, and he looked at her with black eyes glinting beneath thick curling lashes. Tendrils of long red hair swirled around the perfect oval of her face, the neckline of her green gown had slipped a little and exposed more of one firm creamy breast than was absolutely decent. With her body turned towards him and her long shapely legs crossed, an expanse of smooth thigh, was begging to be stroked by a male hand, and she appeared completely unaware of the fact.

'He went back to Brazil and the last I heard from him, he was somewhere in the high Andes looking for some sacrificial burial ground,' Rose added a tinge of sadness shadowing her glorious green eyes. Dominic had fallen in love with her, and on one memorable night she'd ended up in his bed. It had been a mistake, and almost spoilt a great friendship.

'A burial ground seems the best place for him,' Xavier drawled sardonically.

'Why do you say that?' Rose asked in genuine surprise. 'He is a nice man; you would probably like him.' And as she said it she realised it was true. Dominic was the same type of man as Xavier, though without Xavier's ruthless streak. With a flash of insight, she admitted to herself that was probably why Dominic had been the only man to tempt her into bed in ten years. He had reminded her of Xavier! Dominic, bless him had realised her emotions were not involved and had graciously withdrawn from his pursuit of her.

'If you say so,' Xavier said showing his teeth. He gave a curt nod to someone behind Rose and got to his feet. 'It appears our cab has arrived.' He stretched out an imperious hand towards her and something about his stance, the gleaming hooded eyes told her not to argue, and she placed her hand in his.

But he did not need to jerk her to her feet quite so violently Rose thought, almost tripping over on her high-heeled shoes. But with one derisory glance at her lovely face he tightened his hold on her hand and dashed her through the reception and out into the cool night air.

'What's the hurry?' She couldn't help commenting, a slight shiver running down her spine, but whether it was the cold air, or the effect of his large hand enfolding her own, she didn't know.

'Get in the car,' Xavier said coldly, dropping her hand. 'It's been a long day and an even longer night, and I for one have had enough. I will be glad to get home tomorrow. With you and Jamie and Ann of course.'

Why did she think the last sentence had been tacked on as an afterthought? Rose grimaced as she climbed into the car. Xavier Valdespino had come to Yorkshire out of duty. He'd played his part with smooth sophistication, and charm, and he couldn't wait to get away. Rose had nothing to worry about, she would spend a week in Seville with Jamie and Ann. Xavier Valdespino would no doubt be the perfect host. But as for remembering a stupid young girl he'd once spent a night with ten years ago, she had nothing to fear, nothing at all...

On returning to the house she refused Xavier's terse offer of a nightcap and went straight to bed. An hour later she was still wide awake. It was no use; she was never going to get to sleep, and with a defeated sigh she opened her eyes, and let her memory stray back to the past. Maybe if she faced her demons, to be more exact one demon—Xavier, she might finally find the sleep she craved.

* * *

THE HEAVY BEAT of the music signalled her entrance on to the catwalk. Head held high, she sauntered down the runway wearing a wisp of silk. Tiny spaghetti straps over her slender shoulders made no pretence of supporting the bodice that plunged almost to her navel and a hemline that struggled to cover her behind. Her beautiful face was expressionless, her dark red hair cut in a short bob and ruthlessly straightened. Her wide emerald eyes were heavily lined with kohl; the waif look was in…. For Rose it was no hardship to achieve.

At sixteen she'd been spotted at the Birmingham Clothes Show and asked if she would like to be a model. Five feet eight and as thin as a reed she was just the type the model agency was looking for.

Her parents, both doctors, had discussed the offer with her and finally agreed to her modelling, but only in the school holidays. Her modelling name was simply "Maylyn," a play on her own name Rosalyn May, because as her father had pointed out, if she eventually wanted to be taken seriously as a doctor, it would be better not to use her real name.

Glancing around the glittering audience Maylyn was totally oblivious to the enthusiastic applause. Tonight her mind was consumed with the technicalities of moving house next week, and when she was going to get all her packing done. After the tragic death of her parents a year past January on a mercy mission in Central Africa when their plane had crashed killing all on board, Rose had found herself alone except for Peggy, the au pair who'd looked after her since she was two. After talking it over with her Aunt Jean and Uncle Alex, the only family she had left, it was decided Rose would stay in the family home in London with Peggy until she finished her A-level exams. She'd passed with straight As last summer although she'd been weighed down with grief. She'd been accepted by University College London to read medicine, but decided to defer for a year and concentrate on her modelling with the idea of making enough money to see her through medical school.

Last Christmas Peggy announced she was getting married in a few months, and so Rose had put the large family house up for sale and decided to buy an apartment a couple of streets away. Ironically the death of her parents had resulted in her losing a lot more weight, and her career as a model had really taken off, so money was not a problem.

Which was why she was in Barcelona taking part in a few charity fashion shows held in conjunction with the Spanish Grand Prix in the month of May. Personally she would rather be in England with her Aunt and family in Yorkshire celebrating her birthday. She was nineteen today, but looking around the glittering crowd she felt more like ninety. But not for much longer she consoled herself.

Maylyn the model, working on autopilot reached the end of the catwalk and with a swing of her hips she spun around. The tiny slip of grey silk that passed for a designer gown, flared seductively around her thighs and she had the traitorous thought that no woman in her right mind would be seen in public in the thing. But then after tomorrow neither would she. Completely unconsciously she smiled at the thought. Next week a new apartment and a long holiday, then come September, she'd be a student once again. Sauntering back towards the stage she felt the hair on the back of her neck stand on end, along with a frisson of excitement as shocking as it was unexpected. Her eyes widened and she was suddenly aware of a tall, magnetically handsome man standing to one side, his dark eyes fixed on hers with a glittering intensity, his firm mouth curved in a sensual smile.

Oh hell! He thought she was smiling at him! He'd been at the show yesterday and Maylyn had hardly been able to keep her eyes off him. He had appeared backstage after the show and spoken to her.

'Maylyn, I have been longing to meet you. You were brilliant out there tonight.'

With the arrogance of youth and intelligence Maylyn had avoided all the pitfalls that assailed other models. She did not smoke, and she had yet to meet a man who could persuade her into bed. But one look at the dark stranger, and she had lost herself entirely in eyes as warm as hot chocolate. She felt a laser-sharp stirring in her blood and her cheeks flared scarlet. She could not drag her gaze away and in that moment all her preconceived notions of love and morality vanished in a puff of smoke. Deep down inside some instinct warned her this man was dangerous, but she ignored it. Smiling up at him—he was well over six feet—she said, 'Thank you,' in a voice that was decidedly husky.

He offered her a cigarette, but when she refused, he'd said he could get her something stronger. She knew drugs abounded in the modelling world, but she had nothing to do with them. Bitterly disillusioned and imagining he was a drug dealer she'd slapped his face and walked away... Remembering where she was and what she was supposed to be doing she dragged her gaze away from the handsome devil and completed the parade.

'YOU WERE NOT supposed to smile,' the very angry Spanish designer who had hired her snapped at her as soon as she got backstage. 'And I think you are putting on weight.'

Maylyn looked at the small, dark, effeminate man, and smiled again. A designer's ploy for keeping models in line was to tell them they were getting fat but she no longer cared. 'Sorry, Sergio,' she grinned. 'I could not help myself.'

'You are impossible Maylyn; beautiful but impossible,' Sergio declared. 'For once in your life try and do as you are told. Keep that gown on and get around the front and mingle. The party is about to start, and everyone who is any one in Spain is here as well as every racing driver in the world and their backers.'

'Do I have to?' Maylyn groaned.

'If you want to be paid. Yes.'

Taking a glass of champagne she had no intention of drinking from a passing waiter, Maylyn edged her way through the press of bodies. She responded to the countless calls of her name with a brief smile and a nod of her head. Finally she found what she was looking for; a quiet corner behind a large potted palm and leaned against the wall. She slipped one foot out of a ridiculously high-heeled shoe, and sighed with relief. With a bit of luck she could escape in a minute back to her hotel, and glancing warily around, she upended the glass of champagne into the potted palm.

'I saw that. How cruel—you destroy an innocent plant as easily as you destroyed my hope yesterday.'

She dropped the glass into the pot in surprise and turned her head, astonished to see sliding behind the other side of the palm was the tall dark man who had grabbed her attention earlier on the catwalk.

She blushed to the roots of her hair. 'I didn't mean... I wasn't...' she stammered helplessly, her heartbeat quickening as she stared at him. He was even more devastating than she remembered. He had the face of a fallen angel, she thought fancifully. He was incredibly handsome, with the olive-skinned complexion of the Mediterranean male. Perfectly arched black brows rose over deep brown eyes that glinted with a touch of gold. He had a not-quite-straight nose with slightly flaring nostrils, and high cheekbones that most women would kill for. Add a wide sensual mouth, and he was too attractive to be true. Maylyn was tall but he towered over her by a good eight inches. His broad shoulders strained against the fine cotton of an obviously tailor-made shirt, a carved leather belt rode low on his hips supporting cream pleated trousers. He was casually dressed, but she recognised the designer label.

He leaned back against the wall beside her, crossing one long leg over the other at the ankle revealing the finest hand-tooled leather loafers. 'Only joking Maylyn. I simply wanted a chance to set the record straight. I am not a drug dealer, as you seemed to imagine yesterday, I was only trying to ascertain you were not on drugs. I'm afraid my cynicism where models are concerned was showing, and I apologise.'

Maylyn believed him, on second acquaintance he looked far too distinguished to be a drug dealer. 'That's all right,' she said dryly, she knew only too well the public conception of models and drugs.

'I can assure you I work honestly for my living, and I would really like to talk to you again without getting my face slapped,' he smiled and she forgot every doubt she had harboured about the man.

She was totally captivated by his dark good looks, and the rush of relief, the *frisson* of excitement she felt made her lips curve in a perfect smile. 'So long as it is only talk, fire away,' she responded cheekily.

'Well I did have something else in mind as well,' he drawled throatily.

With a real sense of disappointment Maylyn straightened up and slipped her foot back in her shoe. She had lost count of the times handsome older men had come on to her in the past year. She had hoped this one might be different, but obviously not. 'You've got the wrong girl,' she said quietly.

'No.' He caught her arm as she would have moved away. 'Please. I only meant I have not eaten yet this evening, and I would be honoured if you would have dinner with me.'

'I don't even know your name,' Maylyn prompted, sorely tempted to accept his dinner invitation. The man's fingers around her bare arm, set off a tingling sensation in her whole body, the like of which she had never experienced in her life before. His dark soulful eyes seemed to pierce right through the model mask she wore and reach out to the girl beneath, and she was inclined to believe him.

'No.' One dark brow arched sardonically. 'I assumed you knew who...' He stopped in midsentence, his gaze narrowing cynically on her face, and what he read in her youthful open countenance seemed to make him change his mind. 'Allow me to introduce myself, Xavier Valdespino. I am twenty-nine years old and I'm single. Also, I'm Spanish; *Sevillano* to be exact. At present I live in Barcelona to attend the racing.'

His deep melodious slightly accented voice flowed over Maylyn like a caress. He was also quite spectacularly physically beautiful, she thought he might have added quite honestly. And in that moment she decided to throw caution to the winds and except his invitation. After all it was her birthday...

She held out her hand. 'Maylyn, I am nineteen, and I am single. Also, I am English, and I am in Barcelona for the fashion shows.' She repeated his method of introduction, her full lips parting over her pearly white teeth in a relieved smile.

'Does this mean you will have dinner with me?' Her small hand was engulfed in his much larger one, and his other hand fell from her arm to encircle her waist. She felt the electric shock right through to the soles of her feet, but his laughing eyes grinning down at her blinded her to the danger.

'Yes,' she agreed, mesmerised by the glory of his smile.

'I shall never look at a potted palm without thinking of you,' Xavier remarked as he urged her out of the room.

'I've had better compliments,' Maylyn giggled glancing up at him through her thick lashes.

'But none so genuine I can assure you,' Xavier said quite seriously. Their eyes met and fused, innocent green and worldly chocolate, and for a moment the crowd and the noise vanished, and the world stood still.

'Maylyn,' Xavier murmured, lifting one long finger he traced her cheek and jawbone. 'A lovely name for a lovely girl.'

Her stomach curled a spark of heat igniting in her belly, and flaring down to a more intimate part of her anatomy. She was shocked but trapped by the look in his eyes, and slightly afraid. She did not know what was happening to her, she only knew it was momentous. Maylyn opened her mouth, intent on defusing the tension that surrounded them like a force field. But he placed his finger firmly over her parted lips.

'No, don't say anything, there is no need.' His golden gaze swept down the length of her firm young body, and to her chagrin she felt her breasts swell, her nipples tighten to rigid peaks pressing against the scrap of grey silk. She had difficulty breathing, her heart pounded in her chest, and helplessly she stared up at him.

'I know,' he told her, and his hand firmed around her tiny waist pulling her close against him. His dark eyes burned down into hers, and she knew he was going to kiss her. But a man addressed Xavier in his native tongue and the moment was gone… His arrogant head tilted towards the other man and he responded quickly with a smile.

Then he was urging her through the crowd. He was stopped countless times, by various people, and replied to a dozen greetings, but as most were in Spanish Maylyn did not understand a word. It was only as they approached the exit Maylyn remembered where she was and what she was wearing.

'Wait. I must get changed.'

'You look perfect the way you are,' Xavier drawled huskily against her ear.

'But it is not my gown,' she broke free from his hold and took a deep steadying breath.

'Maylyn, there you are. I thought I told you to mingle.' Sergio appeared at her side. 'Is that too much for you to do?' he demanded fussily. 'I want everyone to see this design.' His hands waved either side of her body. 'I have high hopes of selling a slight variation to the mass market, so for heaven's sake darling, mingle.'

'She is mingling. With me.' Xavier's long arm circled her waist once more, giving Sergio a hard glance as he did so. 'As for the gown. Bill me. I am taking Maylyn to dinner.'

'Now wait a minute.' Nobody bought Maylyn clothes and certainly not a man she hardly knew. The man might enchant her but she was not a complete idiot.

'I did not realise you were with Señor Valdespino darling. Keep the gown, and go, go, go.' Sergio was almost pushing her out of the door. 'Enjoy the meal and don't forget. Tomorrow noon, a private show for royalty.' And turning his attention to Xavier he added, 'I do need her at twelve tomorrow.'

Before she knew what had hit her Maylyn was in a lethal

long black sports car with Xavier at the steering wheel, speeding through the streets of Barcelona.

'I meant what I said about getting changed.' She finally found her voice. 'I have no intention of appearing in public in this dress,' she stated emphatically ' It is not my style at all.'

'No problem.' Xavier glanced sideways at her mutinous face, his dark eyes brimming with laughter. 'I have the perfect solution. We will eat at my place.'

'But, but…' she spluttered at a loss for words. She could hardly object after declaring she did not want to be seen in the damn dress.

A large strong hand curved over her knee. 'Don't worry Maylyn, you are safe with me. I promise.'

Rose stirred restlessly on the bed. It was the first promise Xavier had made her all those years ago, and it was as false as the one that followed. With the wisdom of hindsight she realised, Xavier had caught her at a crucial point of change in her life.

After over a year of grieving for her parents and working almost like an automaton, she had just about recovered. The family home was sold, and she was in the process of buying her own apartment. Peggy, her childhood nanny, was leaving to get married and Rose was ready to enter the real adult world, not the fantasy of the modelling world. She was looking forward to going to university and studying for the career she had really wanted. High on confidence, she had walked down the catwalk that night and for the first time in over a year a spontaneous smile had curved her full lips. That had been her big mistake…

Watching the light of dawn shoot rays of light across the night sky Rose admitted to herself. The granddaddy of them all—the biggest mistake of all time, was what happened next. Groaning she rolled over on the bed and buried her head in the pillow, trying to hold back the final memory. But it was no good, parts of that night had haunted her dreams for years, and if she was honest, they had coloured how she looked at the male of the species ever since. It was way past time she got over it and moved on. Eventually she wanted a husband and a family of her own. Was she going to let a stupid one-night stand blight her life for ever? Xavier who had caused her trauma did not even remember her. Face it, she told herself staunchly. He hadn't been that good. Had he?

# CHAPTER FOUR

MAYLYN STOOD in the middle of the large room and wondered what on earth she was doing here. The floor was polished wood and the window was the length of one wall; the view beyond a stunning picture of Barcelona at night. Looking around she realised the furniture was minimal, two stark-white hide sofas and a black marble coffee table. There was an elegant marble fireplace, the only object on it a small silver photo frame. She crossed the room and glanced at the photo. It was Xavier with his arm linked shoulder-height with another man, and a pretty dark haired girl between them. They were all laughing and the girl had a huge ring on her finger.

'Friends of yours?' she queried, trying to make conversation.

'Yes, good friends.' Xavier smiled.

'You have a lovely home,' she blurted, his smile adding to her nervous state.

'You think so?' Xavier looked dispassionately around the room, his glance coming back to rest on her taut figure. He caught her wary gaze with his own, and added, 'Don't look so frightened. I am not about to leap on you.' And taking her by the arm he turned her around to face him. 'I invited you to dinner, that is all.'

'You can cook?' she asked sceptically, regaining the thin veneer of sophistication her modelling career had taught her, while trying to ignore the closeness of his vibrantly male body, and the racing of her own heart.

'But of course. I am a man of many talents.' With a

shrug of his shoulders and hands palm up spread wide, Maylyn fell a little deeper under his spell.

'I believe you,' she said her eyes sweeping over his tall frame her imagination running riot at the thought of his other talents.

'How does a real Spanish omelette and salad, washed down with a fine bottle of white wine sound to you?' he asked a satisfied smile twisting his wide mouth telling her he knew exactly what she had been thinking.

'Very nice thank you,' she responded primly, and he burst out laughing.

'You're priceless, Maylyn!' His laughing eyes beamed down into hers, his hand curling around her upper arm. 'Come on, you can make the salad,' and he led her into the kitchen.

For the next fifteen minutes they worked happily together, and if Maylyn caught her breath as he brushed passed her in the small space she tried to ignore her reaction. But later, when she was sitting opposite him at the small breakfast table with a plate of food in front of her, and he filled her glass with wine, she was struck with a terrible feeling of inadequacy. She had never been alone with a man in his home before, and the enormity of what she was doing suddenly hit her. A strange man and in a foreign country, she had never behaved so recklessly in her life. But one look at his incredibly handsome face, the breadth of his shoulders, and the strength of his arms bronzed and lightly dusted with black hair, she lost every jot of common sense she possessed.

'A toast to my beautiful Maylyn.'

Picking up her glass she gazed at him, he was so devastatingly attractive he made her heart ache.

Slowly lifting the wineglass to his lips Xavier took a sip, his dark eyes lazily scanning the flimsy bit of silk over her breasts. Maylyn took a hasty swallow of the fine wine but she had no control over her body's reaction, her breasts swelling, her nipples straining against the fine fabric almost painfully. Abruptly she put the glass down and made to fold her arms self-consciously across her chest, shocked by what he could do to her with one appreciative glance. But Xavier caught her hand across the table.

'No, Maylyn. Don't be embarrassed.' Holding her eyes with his he added, 'It is the same for me. Only the table protects my embarrassment,' he said with a wry grin.

Her mouth fell open in shock when rather belatedly she registered what he meant. 'Oh my,' she exclaimed like some Victorian virgin, her face turning beetroot red.

Xavier flung his head back and laughed out loud. 'Such innocence, I don't believe it. But you were right about that dress, Maylyn. The gown is strictly for the eyes of a lover and no other man. Now eat up before the food gets cold.'

He was older, more experienced, he could joke about his body's reaction. Maylyn could not. She ate two mouthfuls of food, and then pushed the rest around with her fork. She hardly dared to look at him, because when she did she could barely breathe.

'What is the matter Maylyn? The omelette not to your liking?' Xavier asked with concern.

Her head jerked up and she tried to smile. 'Yes, it's perfect, but I seem to have lost my appetite.'

'You're a model. It is your work this I understand. But you are also a perfectly beautiful girl, Maylyn.' His brilliant dark eyes held hers. 'Perfection that would be a crime to spoil by a foolish desire to slim.' He told her firmly, 'Now eat.' And she did.

Xavier put her at ease by talking about his passion for cars, and she gathered he worked at the racetrack. Soon they were chatting like old friends. She told him some of the funny things that had happened to her as a model, and he reciprocated by telling her his father ran a farm in Southern Spain. He made her laugh as he described his one disastrous attempt to be a Toreador in the bullring in Seville and falling off his horse.

He laughed with her, and she forgot it was her birthday, forgot everything but the sheer animal magnetism of the man. But it was *more,* she thought as they exchanged confidences. They talked about everything and nothing until Xavier pointed out he had never sat over two hours on a hard kitchen chair in his life and suggested they moved to the sitting room.

Later relaxed sitting beside him on a plush sofa in the living room, she drank the coffee he had made, and cast a sidelong glance at his handsome profile. Suddenly she was overcome by a restlessness that brought hot colour to her cheeks. The meal was over, the coffee almost finished. It was time she made a move to leave. He had behaved as a perfect gentleman. It was Maylyn who was having trouble keeping her hands off him. She didn't know what had come over her, she'd met dozens of handsome men in her working life but none had ever affected her the way Xavier did.

Sprawled beside her on the sofa, his long legs stretched out before him with nonchalant ease, he looked relaxed and sinfully sexy. Her fascinated gaze lingered on his legs, and she guessed by the musculature of his thighs that he was a much better rider than he had implied. Heat surged up under her skin at where her wayward thoughts were leading her, and hastily she raised her eyes. But that was not a lot better; her glance lingered on his chest, the top few buttons of his shirt were undone, offering her a brief glimpse of silky black body hair, and she had an almost overwhelming urge to reach out and slide her hand beneath his shirt. Was the hair soft or wiry? Mortified at where her erotic thoughts were leading her she jumped to her feet.

'I'd better leave now,' she said, her voice tellingly husky, as she nervously tried to tug the hem of her dress down. 'It's getting late, and I have to work tomorrow.' She chanced a glance down at him and was stunned by the blaze of golden fire in his dark eyes. He reached up and caught her hand, and before she knew what had happened he had pulled her down onto his lap. 'Not without a goodnight kiss, surely.'

'Please, you will spoil the dress.' Maylyn said the first thing that came into her head. 'It has to go back.' She knew she sounded like an idiot, but with his arm firmly around her waist, her bottom fitted snugly in his lap and his other lean brown hand clasping her naked shoulder, she felt as helpless as a kitten.

'No, consider it a present.' His strong hand trailed teasingly around the nape of her neck bringing her face ever nearer to his, and she was paralysed by the sudden fierce burst of excitement arrowing through her body. His long fingers raked up through her hair, and he urged her head towards him, slowly as though not to frighten her. But the brilliance of his eyes told a different story.

'I can't accept.' Whether it was the dress or his kiss she was refusing she did not know.

'Call it a birthday present.' His sensual mouth brushed lightly over her lips. 'My sweet Maylyn.'

A brilliant smile made her eyes sparkle, and she leaned away from him slightly. 'How on earth did you know today was my birthday?' she asked, diverted from the perilous situation she was in for a moment.

A deep throaty chuckle greeted her remark. 'I didn't. We are so well attuned to each other it must be ESP!' Wrapping both his arms around her he gave her a big hug. 'Happy birthday my lovely, But why didn't you tell me? An omelette is hardly a great celebration, I would have taken you out if I had known,' Xavier said with easy grace. 'But what about your friends, your parents, didn't they want to share the day with you?'

Maylyn's lustrous green eyes blurred with moisture. He really was a nice man, so caring. 'My parents died almost eighteen months ago.'

'Oh you poor thing.' This time when his dark head bent, his lips captured hers in a long sweet drugging kiss, a kiss of comfort and compassion. Her soft mouth opened to the subtle pressure of his lips, and with a sudden husky groan Xavier spun her around beneath him on the sofa, his lips never leaving hers.

Maylyn did not know what had hit her. One minute she felt secure and comforted in his arms and the next she was flung into a maelstrom of sensations she did not fully comprehend. Pinned beneath his long hard body, his large hands cradling her face his lips moved demandingly over hers, his tongue plunging into her mouth, devouring the sweetness within with a hungry passion that made her head spin. Her slender arms wrapped around him, her lithe young body strained against him, he played on her senses like no drug ever invented.

Her agile fingers slid up over his broad shoulders to tangle ecstatically in his silky black hair. She felt as if she'd never been kissed before until this moment, and it was like a lightning flash, a revelation. This was what she was born for. Instinctively she responded with an urgency, a hunger that had been waiting a lifetime to escape. She shuddered with the force of her passion; she did not simply surrender to Xavier's potent masculine demands, she exulted in it and demanded in return.

Finally Xavier lifted his head, his dark eyes clashed with

her molten green, as they both fought to recover their breath. Tenderly his hand slid from her face to her shoulder, one fine strap of her dress was trailed down her arm, and he leaned back to stare down at the swollen hardness of a perfect creamy breast.

'You are exquisite,' he grated, and gently he cupped her breast, his thumb trailing across the rosy pink nipple, his eyes following the progress of his thumb in rapt fascination as the tip rose to a hard aching peak beneath his expert caress.

Maylyn trembled, her eyes fixed in blind adoration on his strong lean face, her small hands tugged at his hair, urging his mouth back down to hers. Her whole being burned with wild excitement, the musky male scent of him filling her nostrils, and she ached for the taste of him.

'Not here, Maylyn,' Xavier rasped, and swinging her up into his arms he carried her though to a bedroom.

She might have resisted, but any hope of sanity returning was lost as his mouth sought hers once more. Then she was lying on a bed, and Xavier was leaning over her, his dark eyes gleaming golden shards of blazing desire, as he slipped the dress from her shoulders, exposing her high firm breasts totally to his view.

'¡Dios you are perfect.' In seconds he had dispensed with his shirt and trousers, and joined her on the bed.

But not before Maylyn had been seduced all over again by the beauty of his naked body. Her shy but fascinated gaze roamed over every inch of him, from his wide shoulders to the broad muscular chest liberally sprinkled with black hair. Excitement bubbled in her veins like the finest champagne, her curiosity forcing her to look lower to where the essence of his manhood stood blatantly erect between hard tanned thighs.

She gulped and then he was leaning over her, his strong

hands divesting her of her dress and trailing on down the length of her legs, removing her briefs, and her shoes in one deft movement. Naked on the bed, completely exposed to his fiercely glittering gaze she gasped out loud, as slowly he dragged the tips of his long fingers sensually back up her legs sending shock waves through her sensitised flesh that made her shake with a hunger as undeniable as breathing.

'Xavier,' she moaned his name.

'I love the way you say my name,' he rasped, his hand caressing her hip, the indentation of her waist and over her breast to her throat. He raised up supporting himself on one elbow, his wide shoulders leaning over her, then his dark head bent down and his mouth found hers once more. They kissed with a wild primitive passion that made the blood sing in her veins. His hand swept over her body, his agile fingers rolling her burgeoning nipples, first one and then the other and then caressing lower over her flat stomach to the soft curls at the juncture of her thighs.

No man had ever touched her so intimately before and for a second a semblance of sanity surfaced, but it was extinguished as his head dipped to a rigid straining nipple and suckled the bud into the heat of his mouth. She gasped out loud, her body trembling in pleasure that was almost pain, and then he soothed with his tongue, sending her heartbeat hammering against the wall of her chest.

Maylyn didn't know such feelings, such cravings, existed until now. She reached for him, her hands curving around his wide shoulders, stroking down his broad back and 'round to his chest. She discovered the hair she had wondered about earlier was soft and curly, and she was fascinated by the pebble-like male nipple buried in the silky down. His body fascinated her. He fascinated her, and all the time she felt as if she was on fire, her skin burned. She could not control her response; indeed she did not want to, as the sensual expertise of his hands and his mouth led her ever and ever deeper under his spell.

Xavier reared over and crushed her swollen lips once more under his, as his fingers traced along her slender thigh and sought the moist heat of her tender flesh, while his tongue plundered her mouth with a primitive rhythm her body ached to follow.

'Please…' Maylyn gasped wildly. She looked up into his face distorted by passion, the skin pulled taut across high cheekbones and the dark eyes turned to black pools of sheer hunger, and she knew it was for her.

'*¡Dios!* You don't have to ask,' Xavier growled as he rose over her and surged hot and hard into her pliant body.

For a moment he froze as he registered the resistance and her muffled cry, but her hands clasped around his back, she kissed the satin skin of his shoulder, and then cried out with pleasure as he surged back into the hot silken warmth of her.

Maylyn discovered the true meaning of sensuality. Her body knew instinctively how to respond arching into him, meeting every thrust of his loins with a throbbing fiery pleasure that had her fingernails digging into his back. Higher and higher she flew soaring into the unknown, her heart thundering, her greedy hands holding him fiercely, terrified he would stop, and deny her craving for the ecstasy she knew was waiting just over the horizon.

Then it happened; her body convulsed in wave upon wave of scorching release as he surged into her one last time. The sound she could hear was her own cry as she felt his magnificent body shudder in an explosive climax.

Xavier collapsed on top of her, his head resting in the curve of her neck, and she lifted a trembling hand and smoothed the dark sweat-damp hair of his head, loving the way he rested against her, loving the heat of his hard body over her. Loving him...

Xavier sighed and rolled onto his back and sliding an arm under her waist he scooped her up so she was splayed half over his broad chest. 'I was the first.' He swept the damp tendrils of hair from her brow, his dark eyes searching her lovely face flushed with the rosy glow of passion fulfilled. 'Why did you not tell me, Maylyn?'

'Does it matter?' she asked levering herself up so she could rest her arms across his chest and look down into his darkly handsome face. 'It had to happen sometime,' she tried to smile, but ended up nervously biting her lip. She had no idea how to behave in this situation; and a hysterical laugh bubbled to the surface.

'Maylyn, it is not funny, if I had known I would have been more gentle, slower.'

'Sorry,' she said in a flat voice. 'As you have gathered I am not used to this sort of thing.'

Xavier groaned, and lifting his hand he smoothed the hair down the back of her head in a tender gesture. 'And you think I am?' he murmured, brushing the top of her head with his lips. 'Well, I have a confession to make—I am not. This was a first for me as well. I have never had a virgin lover in my life, and as for being sorry,' he tilted her chin up to look into her huge green eyes. 'I'm not sorry, Maylyn. I'm delighted, ecstatic over the moon. You are mine, and only mine now and forever, and in a minute I will prove it to you all over again.' His lips parted in a slow sensual smile, his dark eyes dancing with devilment that made her heart expand in her chest with love.

Daringly she reached down and planted a light kiss on his nose. 'Later. I need to go to the bathroom.'

'So prosaic,' he grinned. 'I'll come with you.'

'No,' she struggled out of his hold, and sat up. She might

have lost her virginity but she had not lost all her inhibitions.

'It's over there.' He indicated a door set in the wall opposite with a wave of his hand, his dark eyes lit with amusement catching hers. 'But remember you are mine and soon you will share everything with me, including the bathroom.'

'Promises, promises,' Maylyn teased. Swinging her legs over the side of the bed and finally glancing around the room that had witnessed her gigantic step into womanhood. She spluttered, she chuckled, then laughed out loud. Pulling the top sheet off the bed and wrapping it around her, she surveyed the totally naked Xavier sprawled on the bed. 'Black satin sheets, Xavier! How naff can you get!' she mocked him light-heartedly and still chuckling she walked across the room and into the bathroom.

When she returned to the bedroom having washed all her make-up off and tried to comb her hair, she stopped just inside the door. Xavier was lying on his back, his eyes closed, his mighty chest rising and falling with a steady beat, his arms outstretched, his magnificent bronzed body completely defenceless somehow, and she was hit with such an overpowering feeling of love, she could hardly breathe.

'Come to bed, Maylyn I can feel you standing there,' Xavier said softly without even opening his eyes.

'How did you know I was here?' she asked crossing to the bed and letting the satin sheet fall from her body.

'You're the other half of me.' His eyes opened and captured hers, and the golden warmth in his eyes dazzled her. His gaze slid slowly over her slim naked figure, and then back to her freshly scrubbed face, an arrested expression on his handsome face. 'I knew you were beautiful, but without your model make-up, you are too exquisite for words. Come join me,' and he held out his hand.

Trustingly she put her hand in his, and he pulled her down into his arms, and kissed her long and lazily, his tongue laving her lips and the innermost secrets of her mouth, and slowly they began the dance of love all over again.

A DISTANT RINGING of a telephone woke Maylyn from a deep dreamless sleep. Stirring she moved but found she could not get far as a strong male arm pinned her to the bed. For a second she was disorientated, then memory returned. 'Xavier, the phone,' she said, pulling at the arm holding her, praying she would see the same love in his eyes this morning as she had seen countless times through the night. Nervously she watched her breath trapped in her throat.

'Maylyn.' He said her name softly, his voice deep and husky with sleep, and his arm tightened fractionally around her. Then quickly his eyes flashed open, and a broad beaming smile illuminated his whole face when he saw her watching him. 'So it wasn't a dream.'

Her fear vanished like snow on a fire. 'No and neither is that telephone,' she told him, an answering smile curving her love-swollen lips. He pressed a quick kiss on her mouth, and leaning over to the bedside table he picked up the offending instrument. Maylyn lay back down and studied him through half-closed eyes. He was so gorgeous; she wanted to pinch herself to make sure what had happened last night was really true. Xavier loved her; he wanted her to stay with him. He'd asked her to stop modelling, and she had happily agreed because she was going to anyway, but before she could explain, he'd pulled her back down in his arms and made wonderful love to her. But it didn't matter. Nothing mattered this morning except their feelings for each other. As she watched his face darkened, his black brows drew together in a ferocious frown and suddenly he looked much older and much tougher, and an inexplicable tendril of fear slithered down Maylyn's spine.

He slammed the telephone down and swung his long legs over the side of the bed.

'What's the matter?' she asked reaching out a hand to his broad back. He twisted around as if just realising she was there.

A wry smile curved his firm lips. 'Sorry, darling but I have to go to the racetrack, I don't know how long I will be.' His deep brown eyes lingered on her young face flushed with sleep. 'My birthday girl,' and smoothing her hair back from her brow he added, 'It is only six-thirty, go back to sleep. I will leave you a key for the apartment on the kitchen table and a card with the address.' His dark head lowered and he kissed her quickly, the bristles on his jaw scraping the fine skin of her face. 'If I get back quickly I will stop by your show. Your last show,' he said with some satisfaction. 'Or ring you at your hotel, and collect you.' And, heading for the bathroom he added, 'But if I don't call you by five, pack your clothes from the hotel and come back here and wait for me. Okay?' He vanished into the bathroom.

Maylyn pulled the black satin sheet up over her naked body and sighed dreamily, and in minutes was fast asleep again. She never saw Xavier walk back into the bedroom, and smile tenderly down at her. But she did stir slightly in her sleep, as she felt a kiss as light as a gossamer wing brush her softly parted lips, and in her dreams she imagined she heard a man's voice saying, I love you.

Maylyn studied her reflection in the mirror above the vanity basin in Xavier's bathroom, and grinned. She looked different, her face held a new knowledge and her softly swollen mouth was a dead giveaway, but she did not care! She was in love. 'Xavier!' She wanted to shout his name from the rooftop, her very own Prince Charming. Instead, humming happily to herself she headed for the kitchen. She had time for a cup of coffee before calling a cab to take her back to the hotel.

Filling a cup with coffee she cradled it in her two hands, and breathed in the wonderful aroma, and sighed, a sigh of complete sybaritic delight. She'd never been so aware of her senses. Everything in her world had taken on a clearer sharper image. A delicious languor invaded her whole body, there were a few sore places, but they only reinforced the ecstasy of last night.

She glanced at the small key on the table resting on the address card. The key shone gold in the morning sun, the key to the rest of her life... A glorious golden future stretched before her with Xavier, her lover. She had only known him two days but she had no doubts, he was her soul mate. She picked up the card and pushed it in her purse and palmed the key. She heard the sound of birdsong from outside, above the noise of the traffic. Every sound was more acute; when she heard the sound of a door opening she shot out of her seat. Xavier was back.

Hurrying through into the living room, her eyes sparkling with anticipation lighted on the man coming in the door. She opened her mouth to speak and stopped dead. It was a complete stranger... He was medium height, heavily built, and quite attractive with black curly hair. He was wearing jeans and a white sweatshirt and carried a holdall in one hand, which he dropped at his feet, and on straightening, his narrowed eyes raked her from head to toe. Then he said something in Spanish, which sounded suspiciously like a curse.

'What are you doing here?' she demanded suddenly realising the danger of her situation.

'My English is not great, but I am Sebastian Guarda,' he introduced himself. 'I live here.'

'But you can't, this is Xavier's home.'

'Ah, Xavier,' he shook his dark head and moved across to sit down on the sofa, letting his head fall back and closing his eyes. 'Xavier is sharing the apartment with me for the week of the Grand Prix, and it is not his home, whatever he told you.' Opening his eyes he fixed Maylyn with a mocking glance. 'Where is he? Still in bed and got you making coffee hmmm?'

'No, he has gone to work,' she told him then wished she had kept her mouth shut, it was not a good idea letting him know she was alone in the apartment.

'Work!' and then he laughed. 'I suppose that is as good an excuse as any. Look little lady I am very tired, I have been travelling for hours, I want a coffee, and to sleep. Xavier and I usually share everything,' and with a crude glance up at her he added, 'But on this occasion you look beat, and I certainly am. So why don't you just leave.'

Maylyn blanched as the import of his words struck home. 'That's disgusting, and I don't believe you for a minute. Xavier loves me. He, he, wants me to stay,' she stammered, and as she spoke, she realised how feeble she sounded.

A snort of derision greeted her comment, but then as if realising she was serious the man sat up, 'He told you this.'

'Yes, he is meeting me when he has finished work at the racetrack.' Xavier had promised. Maylyn refused to believe he had lied. She did not want to believe it... But a tiny cynical voice whispered in her head, *What did she really know about Xavier?* Except he was a great lover, and suddenly she recognised the man. 'You're the man in the photo on the mantelpiece.'

'Yes, and Xavier Valdespino does not work, not as you and I know it,' Sebastian Guarda told her with a sardonic arch of one brow in her direction. 'His money backs a formula-one racing team, a hobby for a very wealthy man. He owns a merchant bank, and has homes in Seville, Madrid, and Buenos Aries, where he also owns vast amounts of land.'

She felt as though she had been punched in the stomach. Feeling the key in her palm she produced it like a talisman. 'But he gave me the key to the apartment.' She opened her palm, her mind reeling with shock.

For a long moment Sebastian Guarda looked at the key, frowning. 'He gave you a key,' he drawled softly, and raising cynical eyes to Maylyn's pale face he added, 'And of course you've tried it in the lock little girl?' The mockery in his tone was unmistakable.

Maylyn wanted to shrivel up and die there and then. It was her worst nightmare come true. Stupidly she looked at the key in her hand and she realised it would never have entered her head to try it before she left.

'Xavier keeps a bunch of keys it is a favourite ploy of his to get rid of his one-night stands without any fuss. I should know—he is my best friend and engaged to my sister. But if you don't believe me go ahead and try it.'

'Engaged to your sister!' Maylyn whispered. With dawning horror she realised the picture in the frame she had asked Xavier about last night was of him and his fiancée. Nausea clawed at her stomach, and she swayed slightly, it could not be true, her mind screamed.

Suddenly the man was at her side holding her arm. 'Are you all right?—you look pale.' His dark eyes slid over her scantily clad form and back to the pale face devoid of make-up. 'Come and sit down, you've had a shock. ' And meekly Maylyn let him lead her to the sofa.

'Allow me to apologise for my countryman. I am sorry. I did not realise, you are much younger than the women he usually takes to bed.'

Sebastian Guarda was kind. He slid a comforting arm around her shoulders, and tried to let her down gently. 'You have seen the photo on the mantelpiece, it was taken three months ago. Need I say more?'

'But your sister... Don't you mind? I mean... Well, you know Xavier is being unfaithful?'

His laughter cut across her stumbling question. 'Xavier's family is one of the oldest in Seville, his ancestors were a mixture of Moorish and Spanish. He is a traditionalist, his fiancée must be a virgin on her wedding night, so until his marriage he is not being unfaithful, simply fulfilling his male urge with a variety of willing women. It means nothing to him, and Catia understands this. Though sometimes, as now, I am ashamed of his behaviour. I can see you are not the worldly type, so once again I am sorry.'

Numb with shock and horror, Maylyn could not speak. Sebastian ordered her a cab and ten minutes later she was on her way back to her hotel.

Sergio the designer was delighted with her performance at the noon fashion show, and he told her so backstage. 'Marvellous, Maylyn. Exactly the pathos I was looking for.'

Her great green eyes filled with tears, and she blinked furiously. 'I'm glad someone is satisfied,' she said in a voice that wobbled.

'Oh my God! Valdespino, you've fallen for him, you poor thing,' Sergio's arm curved around her shoulder, his expression filled with compassion on her pale face. 'I should have warned you, rumour has it he is engaged to a suitable young girl, although he is a notorious womaniser. But to give him his due, he is very generous with the ladies in his life. Look on the bright side, one of his staff contacted me this morning, and arranged to pay for the dress, so you are now a proud owner of a fabulous Sergio original.'

Listening to Sergio, any faint lingering hope that it might all be a terrible mistake, and Xavier would arrive at the show, or perhaps contact her at her hotel, died a death. He'd bought her for the cost of a dress. If she had not disliked the dress before, she hated it now.

Back in her hotel room, Maylyn called the airport, and was lucky to get a seat on a holiday charter flight leaving at four-thirty that evening. Hastily she flung her clothes in a suitcase. Tears streaming down her cheeks she tore the dress to shreds and shoved it in the waste bin. Whether the tears were for a broken heart or simply pure rage at her own stupidity in believing in love at first sight, she did not dare to analyse. She had behaved like a naive young fool and fallen for Xavier's lies. Never again, she vowed, and called a cab.

Replacing the receiver, she picked up her purse, checking she had her passport. Her glance lingered on the printed card—Sebastian Guarda and the address and telephone number of the apartment. Proof if more proof were needed that Xavier had lied—he had not even given her his own phone number. The phone rang and she picked it up again.

'Maylyn, what are you playing at? You left the key,' Xavier's angry voice echoed down the line.

'I don't need the key or you. Goodbye.' and she hung up on him. The telephone was ringing again as she picked up her suitcase and left.

# CHAPTER FIVE

ROSE WOKE UP to the sound of a door slamming. Blinking sleepily she began to sit up and only then realised by the strange decor she was not at home. She rubbed her eyes with her knuckles. Had yesterday really happened? Xavier Valdespino was going to be related to her family—it did not bear thinking about. She groaned out loud and was tempted to slide back down under the covers.

'Sorry Rose, but you have to get up.' Ann approached the bed carrying a mug of coffee in one hand.

'What time is it?' Rose muttered, viewing her pretty cousin with bleary vision.

'Eleven-thirty. Drink this and hurry up and get ready, we are leaving soon.' She placed the china mug on the bedside table.

'Eleven-thirty.' Rose yelped. 'Why didn't you wake me?' swinging her legs over the side of the bed she sat up, and reached for the steaming cup of coffee.

'Because Xavier reminded us your boss had sent you back to England to rest, and insisted we leave you to sleep. I think you have made a conquest there!' Ann grinned down at her. 'So thank him, not me,' and with that she left.

Standing under the shower Rose groaned in mortification. A houseguest that stayed in bed till almost lunchtime, and it was all that dreadful man's fault. Stepping out of the shower she quickly rubbed herself dry with a soft towel, and back in the bedroom, she slipped on a clean bra and briefs. Shoving her arms into a short-sleeved blue polo shirt, she pulled on a pair of grey chinos and slipped a snakeskin belt through the loops of the pants fastening it firmly around her slim waist.

Vigorously brushing her long hair back from her face, she mused on the anomaly of the snakeskin belt. It had been a present from a tribe in Botswana where she'd run a clinic for a while and she felt no guilt wearing it. But she would not dream of wearing a fur coat. Hypocrite, she told herself with a grin as she walked out of the bedroom and down the stairs, the lingering traces of her smile making her green eyes sparkle.

'Good morning, Rosalyn. I trust you slept well,' Xavier drawled, his long-legged frame leaning against the drawing room door watching her descent.

Her head held high, her eyes flicked quickly over him. He was dressed in black jeans and a black polo shirt. He looked like a superb male specimen, arrogance in every line of his large frame. 'Yes thank you,' she said stiffly, refusing to be intimidated by his overwhelming masculine presence. 'But you could have woken me up.' She was still seething at the information Ann had imparted. It had been his decision to leave her to rest.

'Now there is an invitation almost impossible to refuse,' he sounded amused 'I must remember that the next time you sleep late.'

Realising what she had said, Rose felt a hot tide of colour sweep up her face, and dashing past him she fled to the back of the house and the safety of the kitchen with the sound of his husky chuckle ringing in her ears. The man was impossible, her mind was made up—she was not going anywhere with him.

Ann, Jean and Teresa were in the kitchen and as soon as Rose entered, a large plate of eggs and bacon was placed on the table and she was told to sit down and eat as they were leaving in half an hour.

Between forking the food into her mouth she tried to tell them she was not going to Spain. 'It's the twenty-first century, nobody has a chaperone nowadays.'

'Please Rose stop wasting time,' Ann snapped. 'Xavier has already called his pilot twice and put back the flight time. East Midlands Airport is incredibly busy this time of year with holiday charter flights all over the Mediterranean. If we miss the next take-off slot, that is it until tomorrow.'

In the process of swallowing a mouthful of the egg, Rose almost choked. He had his own plane, but then why not, he had everything else, she thought bitterly.

'Have you packed?' Ann demanded.

'Yes, no.' Rose muttered. 'My weekend things are upstairs and the rest are in the car.' The E-type—it was a lifeline. 'But I can't leave Bertram,' she declared triumphantly.

A movement in the doorway jerked her head around. Silently, somehow making the large farmhouse kitchen suddenly seem small Xavier walked into the room with Uncle Alex trailing behind him. But it was Xavier who held her attention. He stilled, tension in every line of his body, his lashes dropping very low masking his expression.

'Surely your boyfriend can live on memories for a week in support of your family,' Xavier prompted, his voice deep and with a note in it that hinted of strong emotions rigidly kept under control by sheer strength of will. 'I had to,' he added in a roughened undertone.

She caught his last comment just before the sound of Ann and Alex's laughter filled the room. Obviously he was referring to living on memories of his late wife; he must have loved her a lot, Rose realised and dismissed the pang of hurt she felt as indigestion. Dropping her fork she pushed her plate away. She almost felt sorry for him.

Alex tapped Xavier on the back. 'No, old man, you have

it all wrong.' His laughter faded to a chuckle. 'Rosalyn doesn't have a boyfriend. She is far too involved in serving the masses,' he said still chuckling. 'Bertram is her car.' And turning to Rose, he added, 'There is no need to worry about the car. I will look after it for you. Jean and I will keep it until you return. In fact you will be doing me a favour. I can't wait to get behind the wheel again. Your Dad used to let me drive it sometimes, we had such fun.'

Uncle Alex's reference to her father, and the unmistakable wistful smile he bestowed on her, convinced Rose she had no choice. 'I'll go get my bag and the key,' she surrendered gracefully and rising to her feet she glanced at Xavier as she made to walk past him.

'Good girl,' he said with a brief smile that had driven the tension from his striking features. 'And I promise you will have an interesting holiday.'

She almost smiled back, but common sense prevailed. She needed another promise from the powerful Xavier Valdespino like a hole in the head, and where did he get off calling her a girl, the patronising prig, Rose thought dryly, and escaped back to the privacy of her bedroom.

The fact that her heart was beating rather fast she put down to running upstairs; not for a second was she going to admit it was because Xavier had smiled at her. Her decision made she wasted no time packing her few belongings and dashed back downstairs and outside. Hurrying over to her car she opened the boot and curved her hand around the handle of her suitcase.

'Allow me,' a large masculine hand took the suitcase from her grasp, and swung it out and onto the ground.

Rose's glance flew up to meet dark enigmatic eyes. 'I am not helpless.'

'Did I suggest you were?' he demanded with an arrogant arch of one black brow. 'Any woman, who calls a magnificent piece of machinery like this "Bertram" would have to be reasonably self-confident. It is not the easiest car to drive or maintain.' Ignoring her, his eyes lit up with genuine appreciation of the long low-slung sports car, and slowly he strolled around it.

Rose hid a wry smile. In a choice between the E-type and herself, as far as Xavier was concerned the car won hands down. She had nothing to worry about from the man.

Relaxing slightly, she handed the keys to her uncle, and he went whistling off happily to where the rest of the family stood at the door, while Xavier arrived back at her side.

'The popular myth is that men like sports cars because they are a kind of phallic extension of themselves. It suddenly occurred to me the same could be said for a woman like you, Rosalyn,' he declared with dark eyes that blazed with blatant sexual awareness that shocked Rose even as her stomach clenched in response.

'What?' she exclaimed, captured by the raw magnetism of his gaze. He'd changed in a second from cool sophisticate to something much more threatening to her equilibrium. A wide charismatic smile curved his sensuous mouth that made her heart squeeze in her breast. She tore her eyes away from his, appalled by the sudden rush of heat to her cheeks.

'Admit it. Bertram has to be a real turn-on for you.'

She had just convinced herself he had no interest in her as a woman, and now this… He was doing it deliberately, trying to get a rise out of her she knew. But no way was she going there. 'You're mad,' she said curtly, but she was too embarrassed to look at him, and heaved a sigh of relief when Jamie called out to them to get in his car.

Rose wrinkled her nose up disapprovingly as she sat down in the aircraft seat and fastened her safety belt. Xavier was at the front of the plane in conversation with the pilot.

Jamie and Ann were wrapped up in each other as usual. And Rose was frowning at the pure luxury evident in the private Jet. After the poverty she had seen it was some how slightly disgraceful that one man should own so much.

'Penny for your thoughts,' Xavier appeared sinking down into the seat beside her. his shoulder only inches from her own.

Glancing sideways at his handsome profile and with the slight brush of his hard thigh against hers, she was maddeningly aware of her own weak willed body's heated response to him. A million pounds was not enough to divulge her true thoughts she thought despairingly. Why did this one man have such an electric effect on her? It wasn't fair. But then not much in life was. So she told him her view on conspicuous consumption as the easy way out.

Surprisingly the flight passed quickly as they got into an argument on the distribution of wealth. Xavier was a highly intelligent articulate man and Rose realised she was actually enjoying pitting her wits against his. In the heat of the argument about the western banks wiping out the debt of all the Third World countries, an idea Rose espoused, and Xavier as a Banker did not, her convictions got the better of her temper and she called him a *typical greedy capitalist power-hungry control freak* and Jamie intervened.

'Pack it in, Rose, he is winding you up. He donates to a host of charities, and supports dozens of African students, and heaven knows what else!'

Shamefaced, Rose lifted wary eyes to Xavier's. 'Is that right?'

'Guilty as charged,' Xavier murmured, his mobile mouth twitching in the briefest of smiles. 'But you do rise to the bait so easily Rosalyn, I could not resist.'

Rose swallowed hard. It was her own fault for running

off at the mouth. 'Then I am sorry for calling you what I did.'

Xavier stared steadily back at her, his dark eyes unfathomable, not a revealing muscle moving on his strongly chiselled features. 'Your apology is premature. You were at least half right. I am a hungry control freak,' he admitted in a deep-voiced cynical drawl that left Rose feeling vaguely threatened. Why? She had no idea…

The captain's voice at that moment sounded over the intercom, and her attention was diverted. They were about to land.

LATER ROSE would wonder how she could have been so stupid, but when the airport formalities had been completed, she made no demure when Xavier informed her Jamie and Ann would be travelling in the waiting limousine to his home. She and Xavier would follow on in his Ferrari, conveniently parked at the airport. The excuse there was not enough room for all the luggage sounded plausible.

But once she was seated in his low-slung sports car, with Xavier's long body only inches away from her, she began to wonder on the advisability of being alone with him. She shot him a sideways glance as he manoeuvred the car out of the airport and onto the main road. 'I might have guessed you would drive a Ferrari,' she said to break the tension growing in the silence.

'You know me so well.' His dark gaze flicked to her and back to the road, and immediately she realised she had almost put her foot in it again.

'Well you liked my car so,' she shrugged her shoulders, 'Obviously you are the sports car type.'

'Correct, I have quite a collection of veteran models. They are in storage outside the city. I'll show them to you one day,' he said conversationally. 'But for every day driving, I love my red Ferrari.'

'Why red? A bit blinding in the sun I would have thought,' she asked composedly, because she was keeping such a tight rein on herself. Enclosed with Xavier in the close confines of the car was having a disastrous effect on her senses. She couldn't help but be aware of his strong fingers curved around the steering wheel, or the movement of muscle and sinew in his long legs as he steered the car through the frantic traffic.

'I'm a traditionalist. A Ferrari can only be red in my book.'

Without comment Rose turned her head to look out of the window. He'd reaffirmed what she already knew. She'd found out the hard way at nineteen from his friend Sebastian exactly how traditional Xavier was, and why she should feel depressed at the thought she didn't know. Xavier meant nothing to her. The reason she was sitting beside him in the car was simply another tradition—to act as chaperone to her cousin.

Suddenly Xavier cursed and the car swerved violently to avoid a white van cutting in front of them. 'My God,' Rose exclaimed. 'We could have been killed!' Then she noticed the speeding traffic.

'Welcome to Seville, Rosalyn! The drivers are noted as being the most chaotic in Spain,' he drawled laconically.

'I believe you,' she responded dryly, and after a few minutes of watching the traffic she added, 'Almost every car on the road has a dent in it.'

'Not mine,' Xavier said arrogantly.

'No one would dare,' she murmured under her breath, as the car stopped at some traffic lights.

But he heard and turning his dark head, hard black eyes

narrowing with some fierce emotion captured hers, 'Are you afraid of me Rosalyn?'

'No,' she said with curt authority. She was a mature adult woman, her days of being intimidated by the male of the species were long since over.

'Perhaps you should be,' he said quietly as he changed gear and drove on into the centre of the city.

For a second Rosalyn wondered what he meant, then all her attention was captivated by her surroundings. The roads were narrow and twisting, some had canvas blinds looped from the buildings on one side of the road to the other. Xavier explained they were to shade the public from the fierce heat of the summer sun and if she liked he would take her on a quick tour of the city. She agreed and very quickly realised Xavier was very well informed about the history of his hometown.

He pointed out the famous Gothic Cathedral, Santa Maria de la Sede that had taken a hundred and two years to built. It was actually in the Guinness book of records as having the third largest interior in the world. She watched in fascination as he indicated the Giralda tower, Seville's Moorish minaret, standing alongside the church soaring over old Seville, a magnificent reminder of the city's Moorish history. She glanced at Xavier; his hawklike nose and smouldering dark eyes and jet-black hair, seemed somehow more pronounced now he was back on his home turf. She shuddered slightly, and looked out of the car window.

'I never knew a river ran through the middle of Seville,' she exclaimed in astonishment, as she realised the road they were on was following a wide green waterway.

'The Guadalquivir is a famous river, but strictly speaking what you are looking at is the Canal de Alfonso XIII. The river was diverted at the beginning of the twentieth century to prevent the flooding of the city, enabling the city to continue as a port.'

'But it is miles inland!' That much she knew, her geography wasn't that bad.

A husky chuckle greeted her comment. 'The river has always been a famous waterway, a great inland port. Queen Isabelle chose it because it is so far inland and therefore safer from the English and a few other enemies. Christopher Columbus set sail from here to discover America.' He gave her a quick grin. 'There is an enormous statue of him in the cathedral, supposedly his tomb, one of five dotted around Europe.'

Rose was captivated by the architecture, and the truly Spanish feel of the city. When the car turned off the road and through a huge stone archway and halted in a cobbled courtyard Rose gasped in amazement. It was like no town house she'd ever seen before. Probably built in the nineteenth century, there was a huge wall with garaging and stables set into it which enclosed the courtyard on three sides, with the house on the other. A sweeping semicircle of steps led up to huge iron-banded oak doors that were opened wide. A small dark man was standing stiffly to attention to one side, obviously waiting their arrival. Xavier slid out of the car and she watched as he walked around the front and opened the passenger door for her.

'Welcome to my home, Rosalyn.'

Rose swung her long legs out of the low-slung car with more haste than grace. She glanced up at him and surprised him surveying her with a very masculine appreciation. Her heart jumped and she stood up quickly, her fingernails curling into her palms to combat the sudden fluctuation in her pulse.

'It looks lovely,' she said blandly and stiffened when his large hand curved around her upper arm and he urged her up the stone steps. He said a few words in Spanish to the manservant and then introduced her. 'Max' was apparently the butler come-chauffeur and his wife Marta was the cook.

After the heat outside the interior of the house was refreshingly cool, and incredibly impressive. A mixture of Spanish and Arabic, the floor of the huge hall was a brilliant mosaic, the domed roof a testament to the skill of the craftsmen who had so painstakingly built it. Graceful pillars along each side were covered in very Moorish blue *azul* tiles that dazzled the eye. Behind the columns were the shadowed entrance doors to the reception rooms, and a very Spanish magnificent wood-carved staircase was the centre point.

'My father is resting now, you will meet him at dinner. I will show you to your room.' Without relinquishing her arm Xavier led her across the vast expanse of hall to the staircase.

Suddenly Ann and Jamie appeared at the top of the stairs. 'We are going to explore. See you at seven,' Jamie said brightly descending the stairs.

'Isn't this place fantastic?' Ann cried at Rose as they shot past.

Rose swivelled around. 'Wait.' She was wasting her time they had vanished. 'So much for being a chaperone,' she muttered.

Xavier's lean fingers gripped her arm rather more tightly. 'Oh, I'm sure I can find some way of occupying your time beneficially,' he murmured smoothly urging her to the top of the stairs and along a wide-galleried landing. He swept her along another corridor and past two doors before stopping outside the third. 'Marta has given you the corner suite. I hope it meets with your approval.' And opening the door he ushered her inside.

'My word!' Rose exclaimed. She'd never seen anything

like it. A huge gold canopied circular bed stood in the centre of the room, the heavy silk drapes ribboned in blue. Four elegantly arched windows were set in two of the walls, and walking around she gasped in amazement at the view. One side looked out over the housetops, and to the Giralda tower in the distance. The other had a spectacular view of the river. The furnishings were all blue and gold. An exquisite scrolled writing desk was set between two of the windows, a satin-covered wood-framed antique sofa, was opposite a matching chair, and a low table equally as beautiful divided them.

Slowly she turned around. Xavier had moved and was now standing next to the enormous bed.

'The bed came from a Sheikh's harem. Do you like it?' he asked with supreme casualness, a strange golden challenge in his dark eyes.

'Like it. What's not too like?' she exclaimed, her fascinated gaze flying around everywhere. 'I have seen whole families live in a tent not as big as the bed.'

Xavier chuckled. 'Over here is the bathroom and dressing room that leads to a sitting room that can also be entered from the hall.' Striding across the room he opened another door set in the windowless wall. Rose followed, and gasped out loud.

The walls were lined in thinly veined white marble. A gilt-framed door led into what must be the dressing room Rose surmised, and all the accompanying features were in gold. A double shower, vanity basin bidet, but the *pièce de résistance* was a huge sunken circular pure white marble whirlpool bath.

'Decadent, is the word that springs to mind,' she said dryly stepping back into the bedroom, and finding Xavier was right behind her.

His strong elegant hands fell on her shoulders. She tried

to shrug him off; she did not want him touching her but his fingers bit into her flesh as he slowly turned her around to face him.

'It suits you, a decadent room for a decadent lady... "Maylyn."'

For a split second she was convinced she heard wrong. Her stunned green gaze lifted up to his. His dark eyes glinted ruthless with contempt and there was a menace about the hard mouth and the immobility of his striking features that told her she had not. The colour drained from her face, she could not breathe. He knew—he had known all along she was Maylyn. He'd remembered her. He'd been playing with her all weekend like a sleek black panther waiting to pounce and now he was watching to see how she would react.

After her brief disastrous relationship with him ten years ago, she'd learned the hard way how to disguise her feelings. Years of study at medical school and more years spent looking after the sick and dying, she was adept at blocking out her emotions, in fact it was almost a necessary skill for a doctor.

'The only decadent person here is you,' Rose said stonily. Tearing her gaze away from his she glanced at their surroundings. 'And somewhat melodramatic if you recognised me, why didn't you say so?' She took a step back and broke free from his hold, but only because he let her she realised shakily.

'I could ask you the same question.' Xavier drawled cynically, 'But I know the answer, I could read it in your face when Teresa introduced us. You were as white as a sheet and absolutely horrified.' He stared at her grimly. 'What was the problem, frightened I would reveal the serious dedicated doctor was once a model with a penchant for one-night stands?'

Rose could not answer him. For the past twenty-four hours she'd been living in fear of his remembering who she was. No not fear, in a state of nervous tension, and now he had she was speechless.

'I was watching from the window when you arrived. I thought I recognised you, your hair threw me for a moment, from short and straight to long and curly, and a few shades lighter. But the years have been kind to you. If anything you are more stunningly beautiful than you were at nineteen, and your figure.' His dark eyes slid to her high firm breasts, clearly outlined by the soft knit shirt, and back to her face. 'You have filled out in a subtle but voluptuous way.'

She'd been a late developer Rose could have told him bitterly, as the memories came flooding back of the first few months after he had left her. Her breasts were fuller but her waist was still as tiny. When she gave her shape any thought nowadays it was usually to bemoan her rather luscious curves. 'You mean I am fat,' she said bluntly.

'No.' Xavier curved a large hand quite blatantly around her breast, sending a fierce current of sexual awareness through her.

'Keep your hands to yourself,' she gasped and knocked his hand away, the atmosphere suddenly raw with tension.

Xavier laughed softly. 'So defensive.' His dark eyes flicked down to her shirtfront, where her nipple was clearly defined against the soft knit garment. Then back to her face, his teeth gleaming in a sudden menacing smile. 'When we both know I could have you mindless in a minute. Once I gave you a taste for sex you leaped straight into bed with the next man you met. You can't help yourself.'

The injustice of his comment made her blood boil. 'Why you—' Sheer fury had her hand swinging wildly towards his face, but he caught her wrist and held it in a grip of steel and forced it behind her back, bringing her body into close contact with his long lean length.

'No, my lovely, I am not appearing at dinner with your mark on my face, one is quite enough,' he said dryly. 'But you and I have to talk.'

She closed her eyes and counted to ten under her breath. She was not going to demean herself by arguing about morals or lack of them with the arrogant swine. He did not have any... And if she allowed herself to challenge him over their past association, she knew it would be courting disaster. She would end up howling at him like a banshee. The hurt went too deep.

Slowly, painfully she achieved a semblance of self-control, and opening her eyes she flicked a glance at his hard face. 'If you want to talk, talk. But personally I don't think we have anything to say to each other. We met once a long time ago, but we have both moved on.' She was proud of her ability to control her temper, even though her insides were trembling held firmly against his hard body. She did not know what his game was, but she had a nasty feeling it would not be anything she liked.

He shrugged slightly, his powerful shoulders lifting beneath the smooth black shirt, his austerely handsome face once more devoid of expression.

'As you say it was a long time ago, and the past is just the past. It is the present that concerns me.'

'What do you want?' her mouth was dry.

Slowly his eyes drifted over her, assessing eyes that betrayed not a flicker of warmth. But it did not stop her skin heating where those eyes touched. His mouth twisted in a cruel little smile that terrified her. Belatedly she lifted her free hand and shoved against his chest and began to struggle in earnest, but she was too late as his mouth fastened with deadly accuracy over hers.

She'd been kissed in the intervening years, but nothing to compare with this. He forced apart her tightly closed lips with a ruthless brutality that shocked and yet aroused her. Xavier had lost none of his skill, subtly easing the pressure until the kiss became a battle, a drugging torment that she had to fight with every fibre of her being to resist. A silent moan died in her throat as she felt herself sinking into a sea of sensuality that drained any semblance of resistance from her mind.

Sensing his victory Xavier carefully eased her away from him, and then she knew what real fear was. How could her body have betrayed her so quickly and so completely? She did not dare contemplate... 'I think you'd better go now....' she said refusing to look at him.

His hand cupped her chin and tilted her head back. His hard eyes lingered on her softly swollen lips with a slight trace of satisfaction in their depths. 'What do I want, you ask?' he drawled mockingly. 'You know... What every man that looks at you wants. But I want a little more.'

'You're disgusting, and I hate you.' Her voice was flat and toneless. 'And what ever crazy idea you have has nothing to do with me.' When he had called her decadent implied she had slept with dozens of men, he'd insulted her. Yet *he* was a notorious womaniser. He had some nerve.

'It has everything to do with you. I want you to be my wife,' he told her casually, with no more emotion than if he had been asking what time of day it was.

Her mouth fell open, her eyes felt as if they were out on stalks, as she stared at him completely stunned. 'You're kidding or you're mental,' she grated.

'No, just logical. My father is ill; he has not long left on this world. His last few months will be much easier if he knows I am married.'

'Not to me.' She shook her head in negation, dislodging

his hand from her chin. She was no longer a silly love-struck teenager, she was a mature intelligent woman, and it did not take an Einstein to see Xavier was hoping to use her again, as he had once before.

'That is a shame. I thought your cousin and Jamie made such a nice couple.' Startled green eyes were riveted to his austere features, seeing the mocking twist of his sensuous lips. 'But a little subtle persuasion from me and Jamie and Ann will no longer be getting married in September. No, I think Jamie will decide to wait until he has finished college, and in the meantime, I will make sure he gets a taste of *la vida loca*. He has spent a long time studying—I think he will enjoy the crazy lifestyle for a while. Pity about your cousin, but no doubt she will find some other man to love.'

'You, you...' She could not find a name vile enough to call him. 'You would actually try to break up their rela-tionship?' she exclaimed, the depths he would sink to to get what he wanted was unbelievable. But then thinking clearly she added, 'No, they love each other. They won't let you.' She stood her ground. What kind of fool did he take her for?

'If you want to take the risk with your cousin's happi-ness, then fine.' One dark brow arched in sardonic mock-ery. 'But both you and I know young love is notoriously fickle.'

If Jamie were anything like his Uncle Xavier then Ann would be better off without him. Rose was just about to say as much, when she remembered her conversation with Ann last night at the dinner party and blurted, 'You pay his allowance.'

'I do.' Xavier said succinctly. 'The decision is yours. You agree to marry me, and Jamie keeps his allowance, suitably increased to accommodate his soon-to-be-married state. Something I am sure your cousin will appreciate. Otherwise…' Another shrug of his broad shoulders as much as to say, Who cares? Certainly not the black-haired, black-hearted man staring at Rose with cold cynical eyes.

# CHAPTER SIX

'BUT WHY ME?' she asked almost silently, her intelligent brain racing. It did not make sense. Xavier was the kind of man who could get any woman he chose. He certainly didn't need to blackmail a woman into marrying him. 'You said yourself you're a traditionalist, so why not ask some young Spanish girl? I'm sure there must be dozens who would leap at the chance to become your wife.'

'I tried that the first time. This time I want a mature wife with her own interests, so she will not impinge on mine. A woman who knows the score. I want a mutually beneficial arrangement with no sentimental strings attached. A woman to warm my bed, without pretending to warm my heart. Knowing you as I do, that makes you the perfect candidate.'

He did not know her at all, except once in the biblical sense, and yet he had no compunction in labelling her a woman of little or no sexual morals, he had suggested as much several times. Why, she did not know. But it hurt, and the fact made her angry, angry with herself but furious with him. Her glance flew up to his face, a humourless cynical smile curved the corners of his lips registering a supreme masculine confidence in her capitulation.

His blatant declaration, his casual arrogance fed her rage. 'Go to hell! And take your asinine proposal with you.' She would not dignify it with an answer but beneath her anger there was a growing sense of fear.

He laughed harshly. 'I may go to hell, as you so elegantly put it, but believe me, lady, I am taking you with me. You owe me, and I always collect on my debts.' He was close, too close...

'I owe you?' she exclaimed incredulously, this man who'd caused her more pain and heartache than she would have thought possible had the nerve to suggest she owed him! He was mad he had to be...

Xavier's mouth curled in a smile and her blood ran cold. 'You'd better believe it,' he drawled, the threat implicit in his tone. 'Sebastian told me all about your meeting and how you fell into his arms before you walked out on me. So save the innocent act, it won't work twice.'

'He tried to comfort me.' Unwittingly she was admitting that she had been in Sebastian's arms, but she didn't realise it, she was too angry. 'At least Sebastian was honest, and told me the truth,' she said furiously, her eyes wide with bitter contempt. 'Which is more than can be said for you. You with your hide-bound traditions, and the morals of an alley cat. God help your poor wife, she must have had a life of hell.' She knew as soon as she said it she had gone too far.

His eyes filled with icy anger. 'My late wife is no concern of yours. But as my future wife you would do well to learn some manners.'

'In your dreams,' she flung at him and shivered at the cold implacability in his saturnine features.

'Think about it, Rosalyn,' His hands closed painfully over her shoulders. 'And I'm sure you will agree,' he drawled pulling her so close she could smell the faint musky aroma of his cologne, and her traitorous skin heated where he touched. Paralysed by shock and something more elemental she watched as his head lowered. His mouth was hard and possessive, almost savage, as savage as the fire that flamed through her at his kiss.

She fought to stay passive beneath the onslaught, her

hands clenched into fists at her side, and she would have won, but his mouth lightened on hers his lips brushing gently from the upper to her lower lip, his tongue teasing and tasting until her mouth opened eagerly for him. It was like coming home after ten long arid years. She heard his ragged intake of breath, her body softening against him, and with a husky moan she wound her arms around his neck.

When he took his mouth from hers, and lifted her hands from his nape she cringed at her weak-willed surrender. His hands dropped back to her shoulders and gently he put her away watching through half-closed eyes as the shaming colour flooded her face. 'As I thought; some things never change. I'll be back at seven for your answer, and to escort you to dinner.' He smiled knowingly. 'Perhaps you would like to have a chat with Ann first, I have no doubt she will be all for our liaison.'

The colour drained from her face, taking all the warmth from it. Humiliatingly she knew he was right on both counts. With one kiss she fell victim to his sensual mastery, and Ann was determined to marry Jamie. She watched with frustrated wide stormy eyes as Xavier walked towards the door.

He turned to face her, the cynical aloof mask slipping to reveal a dark intense anger. 'And don't make the mistake of underestimating me this time, Rosalyn. I mean every word I say. I have never been more serious in my life.' And with that parting shot he left, closing the door quietly behind him.

Rose had no idea how long she stood staring at the door. The gentleness with which he closed it was far more threatening than any angry departure, her mind in chaos. She had no doubt he intended to carry out his threat to destroy Ann and Jamie's engagement. But worse she knew he could do it. She liked Jamie and she knew he loved Ann, but he was young. How many twenty-four-year-old young men would be able to resist the temptations a sophisticated man of the world like Xavier could provide? It would not take long for Xavier to drive a wedge between the young couple, and with the added threat of withdrawing funding if the couple did not wait to marry left Xavier holding all the power.

She gazed around the sumptuous room and wanted to weep. In fact tears did glaze her eyes, and brutally she brushed them away. At one time Xavier's proposal of marriage would have been a dream come true. But not anymore…

She had gone that route once before. A month after returning to England ten years ago she had discovered she was pregnant. As she was supposed to have been going on holiday it was easy to hide it from her Aunt. But alone, and desperately lonely, nearly three months into her pregnancy she had swallowed her pride and telephoned the apartment in Barcelona. Sebastian had answered and agreed to tell Xavier she wanted to speak to him urgently, though she had not given the reason. Sebastian had called her back half an hour later with the news, Xavier was getting married the following week and as far as ''Maylyn'' was concerned he had nothing to say to her. Sebastian was under direct orders not to give her Xavier's private home address or telephone number. She began to bleed the same day and suffered a miscarriage that night. She blamed shock and betrayal for the loss of her precious baby, and a decade later the pain still lingered.

Her green eyes hardened. Recalling the past was not going to solve her problem. Rose stalked into the bathroom, a quick look into the dressing room told her someone had unpacked for her. Turning the water on in the whirlpool bath, she stripped off her clothes, and twisting her long hair up into a pleat she secured it with a few pins. She stepped down into the quickly filling bath. A few moments later she turned off the tap, and let her head fall back against the padded rest set into the side of the white marble, and willed her troubles to vanish.

But it was not that easy. Recalling her altercation with Xavier on the plane, she remembered him admitting she was half right, he was a *hungry control freak*. He had not been kidding... Looking back on the past twenty-four hours she could not believe how easily she had been manoeuvred into the position she now found herself in. Xavier was a clever devious bastard, but calling him names did not solve her problem. Slowly she stood up and stepped out of the bath, pulling a fluffy white towel off the towel rail she wrapped it around her body, and shivered. The trouble was there was no solution with the memory of Ann's face pleading with her to be nice to the man still fresh in her mind. She could see no way out, unless she played him at his own game and behaved as ruthlessly as he did!

With a new determination in her step, and her wide full mouth held in a tight line, she dried herself down. In the dressing room she selected black bra and briefs, from a drawer, and then going to the bank of closets, she withdrew a black dress, from the meagre selection of clothes she'd brought with her. A wry smile twisted her lips. Black was very appropriate.

Ten minutes later she walked back into the bedroom and froze. Xavier was standing by a window dressed in a white dinner jacket, dark trousers, a white dress shirt and red bow tie. He looked staggeringly handsome, but she stared at his dark harshly etched profile with unconcealed loathing. 'It is customary to knock.'

'I did,' Xavier pointed out turning around to face her. His eyes swept over her, his gaze enigmatic. She'd left her hair loose to fall down her back in thick red curls. Her dress was wild silk with a halter neck, leaving her shoulders and back bare, while covering her front to her throat, where a band of black beading formed a choker around her neck. The skirt was slightly A-line and ended a few inches above her knees. On her feet she wore low-heeled black mules, exposing her delicately painted toenails. The same colour garnished her fingernails, and her full lips, were coated with a matching lipstick. She had utilised all her old modelling skills on her make-up, a tinted moisturiser for a skin that needed little assistance to glow with health. A blend of eye shadows enhanced her large green eyes and the subtle application of a dark brow eyeliner, plus two coat of mascara to her curling lashes and she was ready to do battle.

'Is the black supposed to tell me something, other than you are a very sexy woman?' Xavier drawled mockingly. In a few strides he had covered the space between them.

'It seemed appropriate for a chaperone.' Rose was equally as mocking. 'Shall we go?' And she was about to walk past him to the door, but he stopped her with a hand on her arm.

'Not so fast. I want your answer. You will marry me?' She had been praying for a miracle and hoping their previous conversation was an apparition on his part, but no such luck...

'Look, Xavier.' She tried for the reasonable approach when really she felt like spitting in his face. 'I can understand you want to make your father happy, but I don't want to get married. I'm a doctor, I have a career.

'An out-of-work doctor at the moment,' Xavier looked amused, 'Sorry Rosalyn but your objections are futile. You still want me, I knew it the moment I spoke to you at Teresa's. You looked at me with wide eyes and the tiny pulse in your throat.' He lifted a finger and placed it over the exact spot. 'Yes, this one was racing just as it is now. I also need a wife. ''Yes'' is the only answer I am prepared to accept.'

Anger hot and hurtful flashed in her eyes as they rested on his dark face but she fought to control it. She had a plan, it went against her better nature, but he'd left her no option, and it was certainly better than marrying a man she despised.

'I am not a whore to climb into the bed of any man who asks,' she said quietly. 'And I am certainly not going to marry you. But if you insist I will be your mistress for the length of my vacation on condition you do not interfere between Jamie and Ann.'

If she fell pregnant in that time, she would have a child to replace the one she had lost. She was nearing thirty and very conscious of her biological clock ticking. She longed for a child, and she had the money to support a baby for a year or two, and as a doctor, she should have no trouble getting another job. It would mean losing contact with her Aunt and Uncle but that would be inevitable anyway when Ann was married into Xavier's family. But on the plus side she would have her own child to love.

'I don't need a mistress, I already have one.' Xavier said almost indifferently. 'I need a wife. Yes or no.'

The sheer naked gall of the man took her breath away. She didn't know whether to laugh or cry. She'd been wrestling with her inner demons wondering what it would be like to have Xavier as her lover once more, planning to have his child without telling him. Served him right she'd thought. She'd imagined he wanted her back in his bed. Now she discovered his mistress already filled the position...

'Let me get this straight.' Carefully she felt her way through her confused thoughts. 'You mean I play the part of your wife to keep your father happy, nothing more.' She glanced at him then and his dark eyes gave nothing away. 'While your mistress takes care of your other needs.'

'Something like that,' he drawled laconically, his hand dropping from her arm.

She stared at him long and hard. 'Why don't you marry your mistress?'

One dark brow arched sardonically. 'You are not that naïve, Rosalyn. A man does not marry his mistress. As a compatriot of yours once said, it only creates a vacancy.'

Why she should be surprised at his callous comment she did not know. He'd kissed her into surrendering to him simply to prove his masculine supremacy over her, while she'd been deluding herself that he actually wanted her. More fool her! He hadn't wanted her at nineteen, how much less likely he would be bowled over by her charms when she was a decade older… His mistress was probably some absolutely stunning young woman who was quite prepared to earn her living flat on her back.

'You agree.' His deep voice cut into her thoughts, she glanced at him, he was flicking back the sleeve of his jacket studying the fine gold Rolex circling his strong wrist with some impatience.

'When would the wedding take place?' she asked, still not convinced, but unable to think of any alternative that would not leave Ann broken-hearted.

'Two maybe three weeks' time. Tonight you will behave towards me in the same friendly way you do with Ann and Jamie. In the next few days we will foster the belief in us being a couple by exchanging the occasional kiss and caress. My father will see the possibility, and by the end of next week I will make the announcement of our wedding. You can leave all the technicalities to me.'

'Do I have a choice?' Rose asked dryly.

His eyes like steel raked her mercilessly. 'Not if you care for Ann's happiness as you would have me believe. But then you are rather good at pretending emotion you don't really feel.'

A bitter smile twisted her full lips. To have a man like Xavier question the sincerity of her beliefs and emotions was ironic to say the least. 'Okay I agree,' she said flatly.

A large hand settled at the base of her spine. 'Sensible lady,' he intoned with a trace of what sounded like smug satisfaction to Rose, as he urged her out of the room and together they walked down the wide staircase.

Rose sidestepped away from his controlling hand as they approached the entrance to the salon. She had agreed to his blackmail, but she was not yet ready to behave as some starry-eyed doting female. She was too angry.

Head held high she swept past Xavier and into the large elegant room. 'Ann, Jamie,' she nodded to the young couple happily lounging side by side on a long brocade sofa. Rose's gaze was drawn to the man rising to his feet from the depths of a high winged-back chair. He picked up an ivory-handled walking cane, and stepped towards her. He had been tall but age and illness had stooped his once broad shoulders. His black dinner suit hung loosely on his thin frame, and the bow tie at the collar of a frilled white shirt that belonged to a bygone age was unable to disguise the slenderness of his neck. One glance told Rose this man was very ill and it was only superb good manners that had got him to his feet as she'd entered the room.

Immediately she crossed towards him stretching out a slim elegant hand.

'You must be Don Pablo Valdespino.' Thank goodness she remembered the name, she congratulated herself. 'Jamie's grandfather, and I am Dr Rosalyn May, Ann's cousin and her chaperone for a week.'

The dull brown eyes set in a face lined and ravaged with pain, suddenly sparkled. 'Excuse me my dear but you are far too young and beautiful to be a chaperone. In fact the mamas would be in fear of you stealing the fiancée.' He chuckled. 'Isn't that so, son?'

Rose was suddenly conscious that Xavier had moved to stand by her side. She glanced at him, and discovered a smile for his father of such tenderness on his usually aloof features that she was left in no doubt he loved him. Much as she hated the thought of being coerced into marriage, suddenly she could understand Xavier's reasoning. She liked the old man.

'You might quite possibly be right father,' Xavier responded. 'But please sit down, and let me get our guests a drink.' And crossing to a drinks trolley he asked Rose, 'What will you have?'

'A dry sherry please,' she responded smoothly but without taking her eyes off the old man.

Don Pablo sat back down in the chair, and glanced up at Rose. 'You are a doctor, but like no other doctor I have seen before, and believe me I have seen dozens over the years. If any one of them had looked like you I am sure I would have been cured immediately.'

'You, sir, are a flatterer!' Rose said with a smile.

'It is all I can do now,' the old man returned with an outrageous wink, and Rose laughed out loud.

'He's a terrible flirt; don't encourage him,' Xavier drawled, handing her a crystal glass filled with amber liquid. She took it from him her fingers brushing lightly against his sending an unwelcome tingle of pleasure through her whole body.

Lifting the glass to her lips she took a sip of the sherry, the liquid warmth of it moistening her suddenly dry mouth. She had to get over this stupid reaction to Xavier's slightest touch, she told herself firmly. He'd made it abundantly clear he only wanted a wife to please his father. Keeping that thought uppermost in her mind she joined in the general conversation with determined good humour.

Max announced that dinner was served and they all moved to the dining room. Rose glanced around, slightly awed by the elegance and wealth on display. The wall hangings and drapes were from another era. The dining table, large enough to seat twenty, was set with the finest porcelain china framed by silver cutlery, and the wine and water goblets were made of the best crystal.

Don Pablo took his seat at the head of the table and indicated Ann should sit on his right with Rose on his left. Jamie sat next to Ann, which left Xavier at Rose's side.

Rose picked up one of the glasses, and was stunned to see the monogram of the family, a scrolled V engraved on the side. How the other half live, she thought once again.

Xavier's dark head bent towards her, his lips very close to her ear, 'They have been in the family for generations,' he murmured reading her mind and at the same time initiating an intimacy between them for the benefit of his father.

'They are very beautiful,' she responded lightly, carefully replacing the glass on the table. She would be terrified to drink out of the thing now in case she dropped it. Not trusting herself to look at Xavier she asked Ann what she thought of Seville.

Everything went smoothly. A young maid helped Max serve the food and wine. A fresh green and nut salad was followed by tender fillets of beef cooked Andalucian style with olive oil and tomatoes, peppers, garlic and onions.

Don Pablo was a witty man with a great knowledge of local history, and a perfect host. The conversation never flagged until Max entered as they were finishing dessert, and informed Xavier there was a telephone call for him. Xavier rose to his feet, and his father stopped him with one word.

Father and son spoke in rapid-fire Spanish, the exchange obviously getting more and more heated by the second, until Xavier said 'Excuse me,' and walked out.

'I apologise for my son's lack of manners,' Don Pablo said with quiet dignity, breaking the lengthening silence, his sallow skin tinged with red.

'Don't worry,' Rose jumped in, she did not like to see the old man upset. 'It is only a phone call. You have a very beautiful home Don Pablo. It must have an interesting history,' she deliberately changed the subject. But it was the worst thing she could have said...

'Yes. The Valdespino family home has been on this spot for five hundred years, the house has changed but always Valdespinos have owned it. Now unfortunately it looks as if the Valdespino name will die out.'

Xavier returned just as his father spoke, he gave the old man a filthy look. 'Please excuse me, I am afraid I have to go out for a while.' He addressed his words to Ann and Jamie, barely sparing Rose a glance, and said something violently in Spanish to his father and walked out.

'You see what I mean,' Don Pablo said with a jerk of his head towards the door his son exited, his dark eyes glinting feverishly. 'It's becoming more and more obvious to me, my son is not going to provide me with an heir. His first night home and he deserts our guests...' Suddenly as if realising he had said too much he stopped, and rang for Max.

'I am sorry I am afraid I must leave you young ones now.' Allowing the manservant to help him out of the chair, he added, 'I am very tired, but please enjoy your evening,' and he departed.

'Phew…talk about drama,' Ann said with a chuckle.

Jamie joined in. 'Forget it. I've seen it all before. My Uncle and Grandfather are always arguing, they are too much alike to live together.'

Personally Rose wondered if any one on the planet could live with Xavier—he was so damn sure of himself; so autocratic he could make a saint curse, never mind his poor father. 'You speak Spanish Jamie, what were they arguing about?' she asked, intrigued by the fiery outburst.

Jamie grinned. 'Grandfather was furious because Uncle Xavier has taken off to visit his mistress. That was who called him.'

Ann gave Jamie a playful punch. 'You better not take after your uncle or I will throttle you.'

Rose knew the feeling, she would happily strangle Xavier herself. But watching the young couple Rose realised she had made the right decision in agreeing to marry the man. Jamie loved Ann and she was not going to be responsible for allowing a reptile like Xavier to destroy the young couple.

After coffee, Rose said goodnight and went upstairs to bed with a splitting headache. It had been a hell of a day… It was okay for Xavier, he was probably comfortably in the arms of his mistress by now… But for Rose there was no comfort as she prepared for bed. Her mind spun like a windmill in a gale. Having met Don Pablo she could see why Xavier wanted the marriage to take place. But God help her! How could she live with a man as a friend when he only had to touch her to send her up in flames?

Dressed in white shortie pyjamas, she prowled restlessly around the huge bedroom, she was too strung up to sleep. She felt a bit like a bird in a golden cage. She supposed that technically, she should have stayed downstairs with the young couple; after all she was their chaperone. What a joke! Xavier had simply conned her into coming to Spain.

She stopped by the window and looked down into the courtyard, as she watched a car swing through the entrance archway, a car she recognised. Xavier was back early from his assignation with this mistress. He stepped out of the car, his dark head tilting back as he looked directly at the window where she stood as if he sensed her presence. Quickly she stepped back, but not before she saw he was minus his jacket and tie.

It was not really early she accepted. After all, how long did it take to make love? He'd been gone two hours. Rose told herself she was relieved he had a mistress, ignoring the hollow feeling in the pit of her stomach. It confirmed what Xavier had said. He wanted a wife who would not interfere in his life, a wife who had her own interests. In time she would take up her career again. Having met Don Pablo it saddened her to admit the man would probably not last the three months she had holiday. Think positively she told herself; by marrying Xavier she could make at least three people happy: Ann, Jamie and Don Pablo. How bad could it be? A long holiday in Spain. And it wasn't as if she would have to sleep with Xavier, and closing her eyes she tried to sleep.

She shifted restlessly trying to relax but her muscles were inexplicably tense. Images danced behind her closed lids. Xavier all bronzed naked strength splayed across a bed, his masculine potency a promise of erotic sexual delights she remembered all too well. The image made her groan, her body hot with frustration and burying her head in the pillow she prayed for sleep.

The next morning, the sound of voices led her to the breakfast room. Xavier, looking uncompromisingly masculine, smiled at Rose as she walked in.

'Good morning, Rosalyn, you look delightful today.' His glittering gaze skimmed over her shapely form with blatant male appreciation. Braless, she was wearing a simple brightly printed red cotton sheath dress, with narrow shoulder straps and a skirt that ended mid-thigh, and sandals on her feet. It was too hot for anything more.

Obviously the open courtship had begun, Rose thought cynically, but mindful of her promise she said, 'Why, thank you, Xavier,' though she almost choked on his name.

'My pleasure. I am only sorry I can't spend the morning with you.' And turning to Ann and Jamie who were already seated at the breakfast table he added, 'And you two of course,' making it obvious where his interest lay. Rose bristled with resentment the mockery in his tone told her he could sense her underlining anger and was amused by it. 'The three of you spend the morning exploring the city but make sure you are back by one. We are leaving for the Hacienda after lunch.'

Which was why Rose was now melting under the midday sun, and completely lost. Seville was a fascinating city; the old town a chaotic jumble of narrow streets that Ann and Jamie had promptly disappeared into, leaving Rose standing in a street lined in orange trees, wondering where she was and more to the point where they were? She'd searched for them for over an hour and she was now hot, thirsty and thoroughly fed up. Striding down yet another narrow street she plodded on until eventually spying a lone woman sitting outside a small pavement café. Rose decided to do the same, and sank gratefully down on a none too clean white plastic chair. A rather rough-looking man appeared and she ordered a coffee and a glass of water.

Her thirst quenched she looked idly around and suddenly realised the streets had become even narrower, and a general air of decay permeated the ancient buildings. A man, a complete stranger stopped and spoke to her. She smiled inanely not having the slightest idea what he was talking about, but when he reached for her arm, she jumped to her feet, and shrugged him off. Time to leave, and she was not waiting for the waiter. She dashed into the dimly lit café and approached the counter to pay her bill, and opened her purse.

How could she have been so stupid? She had a few English pounds with her all coins, but no Spanish pesetas. She tried to give the proprietor a credit card and he made it abundantly clear he didn't take them. She tried to suggest he wait while she found a cash dispenser, and withdrew some Spanish currency, but he wasn't letting her out of his café. He raged at her in his native tongue and the only word she recognised was *Policía,* and she knew it meant police. The situation was becoming threatening.

She hated to do it, but in desperation she finally mentioned Xavier Valdespino, Don Pablo and by gesture asked him to telephone them. The proprietor looked her up and down, and repeated 'Xavier Valdespino' and pointed at her, 'Name.'

'Doctor Rosalyn May,' she heaved a sigh of relief as she watched him pick up the telephone from the counter.

A rapid conversation in Spanish followed and a few minutes later the change was amazing, the man smiled and handed her the receiver.

'What the hell do you think you are doing, Rosalyn?' Xavier roared down the telephone. 'And where are Ann and Jamie?'

'I lost them,' she snapped, not appreciating being yelled at.

'*¡Dios mío!*' You are not safe to be let out. Sit down, and wait for me. Do not move do not speak to any one else. The proprietor will provide you with whatever you want. Understand...?'

'Yes,' she agreed meekly. She did not have a choice.

'Now put the owner back on.'

She could not get rid of the telephone fast enough. A minute later the proprietor had urged her back outside, the seat was wiped down, before she was almost forced into it. A bottle of wine appeared, and a sparkling clean glass. A soft drink was mentioned and to her horror the proprietor sat down beside her. She felt as if she was under guard.

A deep sigh of relief escaped her as a red Ferrari hurtled down the street ten minutes later. It stopped with a squeal of tyres outside the café, effectively blocking the narrow road. The beginning of a smile twitched Rose's lips as the car door was flung open and Xavier stepped out. Her smile vanished at the expression on his face and her eyes lowered. He was wearing tailored cream trousers and a short-sleeved sage green shirt open at the neck to reveal the beginning of curly black body hair.

'Rosalyn,' he said her name, and reluctantly she lifted her eyes to his. The expression in his made her tremble. Furious did not begin to describe him...

# CHAPTER SEVEN

IN TWO STRIDES he was beside her; his eyes flashed with rage, and a muscle jerked in his cheek. 'What the hell do you think you are doing?' he grated furiously.

'I...' was as far as she got.

'Shut up.' Ignoring her completely he spoke at some length to the proprietor finally giving him a bundle of notes with what looked like very bad grace to Rose's eyes, and only then did he deign to look at her again.

'Are you are all right?' Xavier demanded harshly, his eyes raking over her slender frame with analytical thoroughness.

She shrugged 'Fine, apart from getting lost and almost melting in the heat.'

'You're lucky that's all that happened to you,' he drawled cynically, and grabbing her by her upper arm he hauled her to her feet. 'We're leaving.'

Rose gave the proprietor what she hoped was a grateful smile, but inside she was shaking. Xavier was towering over her like a hawk preparing for the kill, his hard face expressionless, but his narrowed eyes were like shards of black ice piercing into her.

His car was holding up the traffic and in the midst of the cacophony of angrily shouted comments and car horns, she was unceremoniously bundled into the passenger seat and the door slammed on her. Xavier slid in behind the wheel, started the engine and the car shot off.

Glancing sideways at his hard profile, she searched for something to say, her eyes dropped down to the open neck of his shirt, and she was surprised to see the scarring that curved his jaw carried on down over his collarbone. She'd never noticed before and then she realised, in spite of the heat she'd not seen him with an open-necked shirt on all weekend.

'How did you get the scar?' The words were out of her mouth before she could stop them.

'*Por Dios!*' Xavier's voice sounded explosively loud in the close confines of the car. 'You like living dangerously,' he said tersely his rage barely contained. 'You know very well, and if you value your life you will shut up until we are home.'

Know? She hadn't the slightest idea. She'd only asked to break the tense silence in the damned car. 'Sorry I spoke,' she mumbled, the sight of his white knuckles on the steering wheel telling her he was still livid.

They drove in tense silence through the narrow streets. Rose felt her nerves stretch like violin strings almost to breaking point. The car screeched to a halt at the entrance to the town house, and once again she was dragged out and frog-marched up the steps and into the cool interior.

'Look.' Rose stopped in the middle of the hall. She was fed up of being treated like a recalcitrant schoolgirl. 'It's not my fault I had to call you because I had no Spanish money. If you had not dragged me to Spain with a few hours' notice...'

His fingers tightened around her bare arm, his dark eyes became coldly remote on her mutinous face. 'In my study,' he ordered between clenched teeth, and a moment later she was in a book-lined room and the door closed and locked firmly behind her.

'So I got lost, it's no big deal,' she tried to diffuse the situation but his hand simply tightened around her arm, and he spun her around to face him.

'Lost in the red light district,' he drawled contemptuously. 'Or like water you found your own level.' His voice was low and dangerous, and she was still reeling at his mention of the red light district when he added, 'What happened? Did the man who approached you not appeal?'

'How did you know someone spoke to me?' she asked diverted for a second from his icy anger.

'The proprietor took great delight in telling me, and demanded I pay for the time you spent soliciting from his bar,' he answered with stark cynicism.

The colour drained from Rose's cheeks 'You paid, it really was a red light...?' She ground to a halt and stared at him, searching the harshly etched angles of his face for some sign that this was a joke. 'No, you must be mistaken, I chose that café because there was a lady already sitting there by herself, so...' She stopped appalled by her own stupidity. 'You mean,' she gasped...

'Exactly the lady was waiting for business. A percentage of her fees go to the café owner for allowing her the use of the table and the same applied to you.'

'Oh my God!' Rose could not help it, her full lips twitched and she started to chuckle. 'You mean he thought I was on the game?' she spluttered, and burst out laughing. The great Xavier Valdespino having to pay for time at a prostitute's table was hilarious. No wonder he was furious.

'Amuse you, does it?' he snarled. 'I wonder if you would find it so funny if the man had not taken *No* for an answer,' and in a deft movement his hand dropped to close around her waist, hauling her hard against his large muscular body. His head lowered and he kissed her. 'What could you do?' he muttered against her lips and as she opened her mouth to protest he stopped her with another kiss.

His mouth was hard and urgent, his tongue delving into the moist interior of hers with devastating results. Her heart roaring in her ears she fought to deny Xavier's sensual demand. His hand moved to curve her buttocks pulling her hips into the cradle of his, making her shockingly aware of the hard force of his desire. While his other hand slid beneath the bodice of her dress, dragging the shoulder strap down her arm, to palm the fullness of her breast, his thumb flicking across the pouting nipple.

Her mature adult rational mind told her to resist, it was pure male animal aggression, but her body behaved with the same urgent need as it had at nineteen. Her slender arms reached up and wound around his neck, and she moved against him, trembling with a yearning, a need she had no thought to deny. She gasped as he lifted his head, and deliberately caressed her breast again. 'Don't,' she moaned shuddering with sensual pleasure.

'Is that the best you can do?' He gave a twisted ironic smile, his hand sweeping from her breast to encircle her throat tipping her head back on the slender column of her neck.

'Try again Rosalyn.'

'I can't,' she murmured, bowing her head, her arms falling from his neck to hang loosely at her side. The imp of truth that had been nudging at her consciousness for the past three days had finally made itself heard. Was she in love with him? She didn't know, but he was the only man she'd ever met who could tear down all her defences with a touch, the only man to make her feel this way. The familiar male scent of him, his hard-muscled body enfolding her had called out to every nerve and cell in her body in a primitive recognition she was helpless to deny. Ten years or a hundred, her body would recognise his to her dying day. The realisation appalled her...

He stopped. 'You can't.' Slipping the strap of her dress back onto her shoulder he set her free. 'You really are a slave to your senses.' He looked amused. 'Well I can see as my wife I am going to have to keep a very close guard on you.'

Anger hot and instant broke through her moment of weakness. 'I can look after myself, Xavier. I have done for some considerable time.' He thought her little better than a whore. Where he'd got that idea from she did not know, but she was not about to disillusion him. Let him think she was a push-over for any man. It was preferable to Xavier knowing it was his touch alone that turned her to mush. 'I suggest you stick to your mistress, and leave me alone.'

He watched her with merciless eyes, she looked away. 'I don't think I will need a mistress,' he drawled cynically. 'Your response just now tells me you are going to be quite enough for me.' Quite calmly he added, 'At least for a while.'

Rose's head shot up at the sheer naked arrogance of his comment. Never mind the fact that she knew he was lying—he'd been with his mistress last night. The thought made her green eyes blaze with anger. But whatever she would have said was stopped in her throat by a knock on the study door and Jamie's voice asking. 'Uncle Xavier, can I speak to you?'

Xavier brushed past her and unlocked the door. 'And I want to speak to you,' he snapped as Jamie walked into the study.

The younger man glanced at his uncle and then at Rose, his eyes widening with the dawning light of knowledge. Her hair was a mess and her swollen lips were a dead giveaway.

'Well, well, so you found Rose,' Jamie prompted glancing at Xavier with a broad grin splitting his face. 'Or did the pair of you plan to spend the morning together the same as Ann and I?' he chuckled.

Xavier reached for Rose and took her arm in a firm grip. 'Go to your room, and pack. Leave Jamie to me.' She noticed his voice held the ominous softness of rage tightly leashed, as he pushed her out of the door.

The door had barely closed when she heard the harsh implacable tone of Xavier's voice lancing into Jamie. She almost felt sorry for the young man. But not half as sorry as she felt for herself. Realising she still lusted after a tyrant like Xavier was soul destroying. It hit at her basic confidence in herself as a woman. She, who over the years had been a champion for woman's rights. Who as a doctor had despaired of women who meekly stayed with men who ruled them, now found she was in very much the same position. To be a slave to one's senses was not something she dared to contemplate.

A very subdued Rose was the last to enter the dining room for lunch. Xavier immediately leaped to his feet and pulled out a chair for her, and Don Pablo attempted to rise to his feet his innate good manners allowing him to do no less.

'Please, I am late,' Rose said sitting down. 'There is no need.'

'Courtesy to a lady was a necessity to a gentleman in my time,' Don Pablo opined, and sank back into his seat with a dry look at the still seated Jamie. 'Though the young seem to forget.'

'That is not all they forget,' Xavier remarked sitting down in the chair next to Rose with a dark look at Jamie.

Obviously the young couple were still in his black books for leaving her to her own devices this morning, Rose mused as she took a sip of the wine instantly provided by the hovering Max.

'I don't know what you're griping about Uncle Xavier,

it seems to me we did you a favour. You got to play knight errant to a beautiful woman,' Jamie said cheekily.

Unfortunately Don Pablo insisted on an explanation and to Rose's horror Jamie recounted her folly of the morning in lurid detail amid much amusement. Don Pablo's wrinkled face creased in a broad smile, his old eyes twinkling on Rose's face and then he said something in Spanish that made Xavier and Jamie look at her, and they all burst out laughing.

Rose felt the colour surge up her face, she didn't appreciate being the butt of male humour, especially when she hadn't understood what had been said. 'What did you have to tell Jamie for?' she demanded in an angry aside to Xavier.

'Unusually my anger got the better of me, and I told him in no uncertain terms, my opinion of a man who would leave a woman unprotected and the unfortunate consequences of such a dereliction of duty,' he informed her in a low tone, and sat watching her an oblique smile curving the corners of his mouth. 'How was I to know he would repeat it?' With a shrug of his broad shoulders he added, 'Forgive me.'

Aware Don Pablo was watching the exchange with interest she took another gulp of wine, and replied sweetly. 'Yes, of course.'

Lunch was horrendous. Xavier threw himself into the role of would-be suitor with a skill and ardour that left her speechless. His cold dark eyes suddenly turned warm and slumberous every time he looked at her while Rose alternated between blushing scarlet and cold fury. When she felt a large warm hand stroke her thigh under the table, she almost jumped out of her skin. It was only by a massive strength of will she resisted flinging the contents of her glass in his wickedly grinning face.

* * *

'IT'S A BEAUTIFUL HOUSE, and the lake is like a mirage,'
Rose remarked to Ann later that evening sitting at the back
of the long single-storied building, on a circular bench that
surrounded a huge jacaranda tree on a wide terrace. Below
was another terrace and another and then the waters of a
gem of a small lake lapped against the shore. The journey
to the hacienda had been accomplished with no trouble. To
Rose's relief she had travelled in the large specially ap-
pointed people carrier with Don Pablo, Max and his wife,
and Ann. Xavier and Jamie had used the Ferrari.

'Yes, nice for a rest, but a bit quiet for me,' Ann murmured. 'Jamie reckons there isn't a decent shop or anything
much within miles.'

'Poor you,' Rose mocked lightly, beginning to relax a
little for the first time in three days.

Jamie and Xavier were in the front courtyard playing
football with some of the staff. Don Pablo had retired for
the night tired from the journey—he was going to eat in
his room. Consequently dinner was to be served at the more
Andalucian time of ten.

Ann leaned forward slightly, her pretty face wearing an
expression of some seriousness. 'Poor me,' she repeated. 'I
don't think I have anything to worry about Rose. But you
could be in imminent danger of getting hurt. I know I told
you to be nice to Xavier, but well… I've seen the way he
looks at you, and Jamie told me he caught the pair of you
locked in the study doing heaven knows what. I know
you're older than I am, and have seen more of the world,
but you've never really bothered with men before. After
years spent abroad in the desert or whatever, you could be
vulnerable to a man like Xavier.'

'It's all right. I know what I am doing,' Rose said softly,
immeasurably touched by Ann's concern. Thank heaven for
the darkness, she thought as her eyes filled with tears. But

Ann's concern only confirmed what she already knew. Rose had to go along with whatever Xavier wanted. She slipped an arm around her cousin and squeezed, Ann cared about her, and would probably have done the same for her. 'I am a big girl you know, and not so naive as you seem to think.'

Ann grinned. 'Thank heaven for that. Jamie and I almost had an argument over it. He said you could look after yourself. But I said any man who has a mistress should not be flirting with other women, I mean Xavier is a widower, so why not bring his girlfriend home? It doesn't make sense.'

Rose chuckled suddenly feeling rather old. Ann was not as worldly as she thought, and she gave the girl another hug, before glancing at her wristwatch. She rose to her feet. 'Come on, its almost dinner time.'

Xavier was the perfect host over dinner. Without Don Pablo's presence, the meal took on a less formal air. It could not do much else with Jamie and Ann so open and happy in their love for each other.

Champagne was served; according to Xavier a tradition they upheld every time they returned to the country after staying in Seville. Yet another tradition Rose scowled. For a man who liked fast cars and fast women, and was perceived by the world at large as one of the most successful dynamic businessmen around, it was amazing his personal morality was a throw-back to the Moors and given half a chance the harem...

'To young love,' Xavier smiled with lazy humour and lifted a flute of champagne to Jamie and Ann. 'Long may it flourish.' But when his glance slid to Rose she saw the lazy humour was tinged with an explicit warning just for her.

Twisting her lips in what she hoped was a benign smile she joined in the toast, 'To Ann and Jamie.' Lifting her glass she took a long swallow. But she'd got Xavier's silent message. The romance would only flourish if she did as he wanted. Rose ate little and blamed her lack of appetite on the heat, but in reality it was more to do with Xavier's intimidating presence. Her stomach was tied up in knots with tension.

Xavier was at his most solicitous, his dark eyes warm and intimate whenever they rested on her, which was pretty much all the time. It became increasingly difficult for her to retain an aura of friendly interest, and when he let his fingers trail down the length of her bare arm, she could not prevent a slight trembling in the hand that hastily lifted the glass of champagne to her mouth. She allowed Xavier to refill her glass without keeping count, and by the time the meal reached the coffee stage the wine had helped dull her senses as well as an inexplicable ache in her heart.

'Excuse us, we are going for a walk,' Jamie was the first to rise from the table with Ann at his side.

Feeling amazingly floaty and slightly euphoric Rose grinned, 'Oh no you don't—I am the chaperone remember.' Standing up she swayed slightly. 'I'm coming with you.'

'No way,' Xavier chuckled, and getting to his feet he put a restraining hand on her arm. 'Leave the lovebirds alone, Rosalyn, and allow me to escort you to your room.'

'This from the man who demanded I come to Spain as a chaperone!' Rose glanced sideways at him. 'You've changed your tune,' she prompted belligerently.

'No, simply bowing to the inevitable, as will you,' Xavier drawled evenly, as he slowly turned her to face him. His close proximity, his hand on her arm, sent butterflies in her stomach fluttering like mad. He tilted her chin slightly with one long finger, his dark eyes narrowed on her lovely face. Even in her less than sober state Rose recognized the hint of warning in the inky depths of his irises. Suddenly weariness hit her, and she barely raised a smile when Jamie escorted Ann out of the room with the laughing comment, 'I trust you Uncle Xavier to look after Rose— she looks a bit the worse for wear.'

'Cheeky devil!' Rose mumbled. 'It must run in the family.' But she made no demur as Xavier slipped an arm around her shoulder.

'Bed for you, Rosalyn.' Faint alarm flickered over her expressive features before she successfully masked it. Xavier smiled grimly, 'On your own...for now.'

The next morning Rose woke with a splitting headache and a hazy memory of gentle hands divesting her of her clothes and lying her gently on a large bed, cool cotton sheet being carefully placed over her body, and the fleeting touch of warm lips on her brow.

'Oh, no!' she groaned, she had a very low tolerance to alcohol and usually stuck to one or two glasses of wine at most. Woefully, she struggled out of bed, made her way to the *en suite* shower room and stood beneath a freezing spray until she felt halfway normal. She dried her hair haphazardly with the wall-mounted hair dryer and left the bathroom.

Back in the bedroom she dressed quickly in white shorts and a blue cropped top. She opened the French windows that led out onto a wide terrace and let in the full force of the morning sun. For a second she was blinded by the light, and blasted by the heat. Slowly her eyes adjusted and she drew in a deep breath of the heady fresh air.

Her bedroom was on the back of the house that faced out over the terraced gardens and to the lake beyond. As she watched a flock of wading birds rose from the water and circled in formation before heading off to the distant hills. She sighed and wished she could join them, before turning back into the room. She sat down on the side of the bed and proceeded to try and brush the tangles out of her hair. She really should get it cut, she thought for the umpteenth time, when a knock sounded on her bedroom door.

'Come in.' It was probably Ann coming to tell her what a fool she had made of herself, she grimaced. 'Don't say anything I know...' She turned slightly and her mouth fell open. It was not Ann, but Xavier...

He walked towards her a silver tray bearing a pot of coffee, milk jug, sugar bowl, and two cups in his large hands. He should have looked servile, but the opposite was true. He looked as if he was lord of the universe, the sun gleaming on the silver in his thick black hair, and glancing off his perfectly sculptured features like a bronzed god, she thought fancifully. She couldn't help it; her eyes lingered on the breadth of his shoulders and the musculature of his wide chest perfectly outlined by a clinging black T-shirt. A shirt that was tucked into the waistband of very old denim shorts, the faded patches drawing attention to his masculine attributes with a devastating effect on her libido.

Her pulse beat a crazy rhythm throughout her body, and as her glance slid down over his long legs she almost groaned. She dragged her eyes away from the tanned muscular limbs with the lightest dusting of dark hair, and ran her tongue over suddenly dry lips. 'What do you want?'

It had not been a sensible comment to make. He placed the tray on the bedside table and stood looking down at her, his chiselled features as hard as stone, while a savage sensual smile played around his mouth. He projected a raw virility that was as electrifying as it was mesmerising to Rose and she could not prevent a swift indrawn breath or the involuntary tremble in her hand that had the brush dropping from her fingers. She recovered quickly enough and when she would have picked up the brush he beat her to it.

'Oh, I think you know,' he said, his smile deepening as he leaned forward and ran a casual insulting hand from the curve of her jaw down the long elegant length of her throat and then 'round to the nape of her neck his fingers tightening on the smooth skin.

His touch burned like fire, and yet his grip was not painful. Looking up into his dark eyes she held her gaze steady. 'Can I have my hairbrush please?' and waited.

'So cool.' He raised his brows, and straightened up, his eyes resting thoughtfully on her proud face. 'Perhaps that's best for now. Pour the coffee, and I'll attend to your hair.' She wanted to object, but he sat down beside her and gently ran the brush down the long tangle of her hair. 'Your hair is magnificent, like rich red wine with the occasional glint of gold.'

'Too much sun; it dries it out and streaks it.' She was babbling she knew. But with his hand on her shoulder holding her steady while his other gently drew the brush through her hair, she was so intensely aware of his scent, the heat of him, she wanted to lean back against the hard wall of his chest, and for a second she almost did.

'That's enough,' she said between her teeth, jerking forward and wincing as the action pulled her hair.

He laughed and cupping the back of her head he turned her face towards him, 'Enough is not a word I can ever see myself using in relation to you, Rosalyn.' He bent and kissed her.

The pressure of his mouth and the sudden heated response that arced through her completely overwhelmed her common sense. A slight pressure of his hand on her shoulder and she was tumbled down onto the bed, his large body following her down, never breaking the kiss. One long leg nudged hers apart, and he settled between her thighs, and all the while the kiss went on. His teeth nipped her lower lip, and then soothed with the sensual lick of his tongue. His lips teased and toyed with her mouth, nipping, brushing and thrusting deep, until Rose helplessly succumbed to the controlled hunger of his passion.

His hand slid from her head and stroked down her throat creating ripples of sensation burning through her body. His knowing fingers pressed lightly on the tiny pulse that throbbed there, as though testing her reaction. She felt the smile against her lips, and then she gasped as his hand snaked lower to rest over the smooth curve of her breast.

Waves of sensation crashed through her control, and she curled her feet around his lower legs, her back arching her body thrusting against the hard, hot, heat of his arousal. She wanted him. She wanted him to cure the burning fiery ache in her loins.

His fingers gripped the bottom of the cropped top she was wearing and pushed it up over her breasts, and then those same fingers plucked the straining peak of one breast with delicate expertise before moving to the other.

He raised his head, he was smiling, a flame of pure male satisfaction gleaming in his dark eyes, and something more, a devilish desire, a promise of sensual delight to come.

Sensuality had long since overcome sense, and she wanted him naked. Feverishly Rose's trembling hand pulled at his T-shirt, her fingers burrowing beneath to the flat plane of his stomach. Her hand stroked up over his ribcage and she heard him catch his breath on a ragged groan. Then suddenly he reared back, and stood up…

'No.'

No, what did he mean 'no.' Rose lay on the bed and stared up at him. He was tucking his shirt firmly back in his shorts, but her dazed gaze took in the fact he was still highly aroused.

'Straighten yourself up, and I'll pour the coffee.'

Struggling to a sitting position, Rose pulled her top down over her aching breasts, fierce colour scalding her face. She should have called a halt as soon as he touched her. It was humiliating to realise she had no defence against the man. While he was a supremely sophisticated devil, with a wealth of experience in the sexual stakes, and able to turn the pressure on and off at will.

Stubborn determination got her to her feet, the colour fleeing her skin leaving her unnaturally pale. 'Don't bother, it will be cold by now,' she said lightly, matching him for sophistication and headed for the door. 'I'll get a fresh cup in the kitchen.'

'Good idea,' he said softly, striding past her and courteously opening the bedroom door.

Rose walked past him, her gaze carefully averted from his dark mocking eyes. Then suddenly she was brought to an abrupt halt as Xavier grabbed her wrist. 'Let go…'

He cut in, 'Wait Rosalyn, your hair.' Reaching out he brushed a thick swathe of hair from her face. 'It's a bit of a give-away—I suggest you do something with it before meeting the rest of the household.'

But his warning was too late, and disaster struck…

# CHAPTER EIGHT

As THEY STOOD in the entrance to the bedroom, Don Pablo was not six feet away sitting in a wheelchair with Max behind him guiding it down the corridor. Taking one amazed look at Rose, with her hair in tangled disarray falling over her shoulders, and then at his son who had one hand gripping her waist, and the other in her hair, Don Pablo jumped to the obvious conclusion.

For a dying man he bellowed like a bull: 'Xavier! You dare to seduce a girl—a guest in our house!' His face red with anger he reverted to his native tongue and raged at his son in a tirade of abuse that appeared to be liberally sprinkled with curses even to Rose's untutored ears.

Her professional persona took over. Worried at what the anger would do to the state of the old man's health, Rose intervened. 'Please Don Pablo, don't excite yourself,' she tried to placate him. 'It isn't…' Was as far as she got as long fingers dug into the flesh of her waist, and she bit down a yelp of pain.

'Leave it to me,' Xavier cut in firmly. Leave what to him? Rose shot him a scathing glance, couldn't the unfeeling swine see how he had upset his father, but he avoided her eyes, and continued, 'What Rose was about to say, father, was: *"it isn't as bad as it appears."* Because she has done me the great honour of consenting to be my wife.'

Appalled, Rose stared at him. She opened her mouth to deny it, but the increased pressure from the hand at her

120

waist combined with the implacable set to his impressive features, stopped the words in her throat.

Don Pablo's startled glance slid between his son and Rose a couple of times, finally resting on Rose's now scarlet face. 'My dear, dear girl I am delighted,' he said with genuine emotion, his lined face lit with a wondrous smile. Glancing down at the old man Rose saw his eyes were wet with tears of joy. 'I never thought I would live to see this day.' He reached a frail hand out towards her. 'Come give me a kiss.'

She flicked a blistering look at Xavier, his lips quirked in a challenging smile daring her to deny the old man. She bit her lip. What choice did she have? Now or next week wasn't going to make much difference. Turning her attention back to Don Pablo, she took hold of the hand he was offering, and bowing her head she pressed a swift kiss on his wrinkled cheek. Bowing to the inevitable sprang to mind...

'Now that wasn't *too* painful,' Xavier drawled mockingly, after Max and his father had departed in great haste for the nearest telephone to spread the news.

'If you take your fingers out of my waist I might agree.' The deed was done; there was no point in arguing, but his large hand idly massaging her flesh was a different proposition. Her pulse beat an erratic rhythm through her body, she pulled away, fighting to control her treacherous senses. 'I still need a coffee.'

'You also need a ring.'

'I don't need a ring.' She was still arguing the point five minutes later standing in the middle of his study, a steaming cup of coffee in her hand provided by the maid on Xavier's instructions. Rose studied him as he withdrew something from the wall safe, her gaze slipping furtively to his firm male buttocks and long tanned muscular legs. Xavier wearing shorts should be banned as detrimental to the health of the female population, Rose groaned.

Without warning he spun around, and caught her staring, and in one lithe stride he was beside her. His dark eyes gleamed with sardonic humour, 'The ring and the wedding first I think.' He knew exactly what she'd been thinking.

In an attempt to regain control of her wayward thoughts Rose slowly drained the contents of her coffee cup, and then placed it down on a convenient table. 'Look Xavier, let's get one thing straight. This is an arranged marriage, nothing more. I... I.' she stuttered and lost her nerve. 'I don't want any repetition of what happened earlier between us.' In other words no sex.

'You will get no argument from me.' His eyes were dark, enigmatic, yet with a brief glint of something else less easy to define. Anyone but Xavier, and she would have thought it was wariness as though he was not quite so confident as he appeared. 'This was my mother's ring, and I want you to wear it.'

Her eyes flashed to the open ring box in his hand, and lingered on the magnificent square-cut emerald surrounded by diamonds nestling in the ruby velvet. Her chin lifted fractionally as she boldly raised her eyes to his. It was exquisite, but she was not going to tell him that. 'Did your wife like it?' she demanded bluntly.

'My late wife chose her own ring,' he responded silkily. 'You have no choice,' and catching her hand slipped the ring on to the third finger of her left hand. 'A perfect fit, my father will be pleased.'

Anger bubbled up inside her. He was right again, damn him! She had no choice. Rose glanced at the jewel on her finger, and she knew she was not prepared to force the issue. 'All right, I will wear it for your father's sake, and it will add weight to the pretence I suppose,' she conceded grudgingly.

'So docile Rosalyn,' he gave her an ironic grin. 'I wonder how long you can stay that way.' Before she'd guessed his intention his arms imprisoned her and he kissed her.

Rose was so furious she could barely breathe when he finally let her go. 'What did you do that for? There is no one here to see us.'

'If you pardon the cliché—because you look so beautiful when you're angry.' His grin was an open taunt at her mutinous expression.

'We will never make it to the wedding,' she flung incautiously, her angry green eyes roaming over his splendid muscled frame that held more than a hint of ruthless power. A power she could not help trying to defy. 'Someone is bound to twig.'

'Twig.' His dark brows rose quizzically. 'Twig, as in tree?'

For once she'd stumped him... no pun intended, she thought smiling inwardly and murmured, 'Yes.'

'Ah! You think the family will find us wooden,' he surmised.

Something about the way he spoke with a trace of accent and his arrogant conclusion made her lips twitch. She tried to smother the laughter that bubbled in her throat, but it broke free, and she laughed out loud.

'I am glad I amuse. The sound of your laughter is a delightful change from the frowning countenance you usually present to me.' Xavier smiled, his dark eyes crinkling at the corners in a cheerful happy grin that made him look a decade younger, and touched her heart. 'How about we saddle up a couple of horses and I will show you something of your new home, while you are in the mood to enjoy it.'

After changing into a pair of cream chinos, Rose met

Xavier in the hall. He'd also changed his shorts for hip-hugging black trousers, and with a broad-brimmed hat held by a cord around his throat he looked devastatingly attractive and slightly dangerous. Rose wondered how it was possible to hate the man, and yet be so vitally totally aware of him that it bordered on pain, at one and the same time.

'You need a hat.' Xavier produced a broad-brimmed cream hat from the hall table and unceremoniously plonked it on her head. 'Your skin is too pale for our midsummer heat.' Then, picking up a square package from the same table he added. 'For our lunch.'

The stable block and barns were a short walk down to the right of the Hacienda. A wizened little man appeared leading a gentle-looking chestnut mare. Xavier waited while she mounted, and assured she was safe. Then the little man led out an evil-eyed black stallion and Xavier placed the package in its saddlebag.

Rose watched as Xavier mounted with lithe grace. Man and beast made a perfect pair, she thought and wished the same could be said of her, as the mare meekly followed the stallion.

Out of the stable yard and paddock, Xavier halted and turned in the saddle, his dark eyes gleaming in the sunlight. His gaze swept from the top of her head down over her elegant torso to her long legs gripping the body of the horse.

'You look good mounted; you really can ride,' he drawled with a devilish lift of one eyebrow. 'Let's go.' Flashing her a blatant roguish grin, he spun around and with the lightest pressure of his muscular thighs he urged his horse into a gallop.

The years rolled back and for a moment she was reminded of the much younger Xavier she'd first met, and her heart lurched in her chest. The transformation from domineering arrogant tycoon to a dare devil cowboy was so unexpected Rose grinned and gave her horse a gentle nudge with her heel and followed.

It was a brilliant clear day. The sun shimmered in a hot haze, turning the surface of the lake into a sparkling diamond blaze that dazzled the eye. Her spirits lifted as they galloped across the hard earth, and later when they dismounted and secured the horse's reins around the branch of a tree, they shared a picnic prepared by Marta.

Rose looked around with wide-eyed appreciation. 'This is a beautiful part of the country,' she murmured idly. Replete with wine and food she sat with the trunk of a tree for a backrest, feeling about as relaxed as it was possible to be in Xavier's intimidating company. 'I am amazed you ever want to leave here.' In the distance she could see acres of olive groves intercepting the rolling acres of sun-baked earth. Surprisingly, there was a section devoted to sunflowers, reminiscent of France, another where cattle grazed and the far horizon was a rugged mountainous outline.

Xavier sprawled on the grass beside her; his head propped on one hand he looked up at her. 'I very rarely do, and then only on business. With modern technology I can oversee the bank and most of my other interests from home.'

'I see.' She didn't at all, he was a renowned playboy, or at least he was when she'd known him. She frowned, maybe his great love for his late wife cured him, but she doubted it.

His eyes were keen and searching on her lovely face. 'I get the impression you don't believe me.' His free hand fell apparently casually over her thigh. 'Am I right?'

She felt the imprint of his every finger through the fabric of her chinos, his closeness, the unique male scent, the powerful intoxicating heat from his body touched an answering chord in her. It was so hard to fight the quick flare of desire his touch evoked, and suddenly the relaxed lazy atmosphere of the past few hours dissolved into an electric tension.

Her analytical mind told her it was simply a natural chemical reaction between a virile man and a fertile woman. But her common sense told her that to give in to the basic urges of the flesh with Xavier was a route to hell: that would destroy her.

Rose scrambled to her feet. 'Believe you? In your dreams!' she snorted inelegantly. 'What I feel or think is of no importance to you, never was.' Her stormy green eyes flicked over his long muscular body sprawled in the grass, and in a voice tinged with a bitterness she couldn't quite disguise she added, 'We have a business arrangement and before I walk down the aisle with you I want it in writing: a legal contract that you will make adequate provision for Jamie and Ann, or there is no deal.'

His face was taut, his black eyes flashed with a devilish light, before long lashes lowered masking his expression, and he sprang to his feet. 'But of course, I would expect no less from you.' Gathering up the remains of the picnic he strolled to where the horses were tethered, angry tension oozing from every pore. He stuffed the remains of their lunch in the saddlebag. 'Shall we go?' And without waiting for her answer he swung up into the saddle. He stared down at her, his expression set, his cutting gaze contemptuous.

TWO WEEKS LATER, Rose stood in front of the long mirror in her bedroom. She decided she might look like a bride, with her red hair swept up in a mass of curls, and framed with a coronet of flowers. Her dress—smooth ivory satin sculptured to fit her tall elegant figure—emphasised her slender waist, and hugged her hips. Classic in its simplicity, the skirt slid sleekly over thigh and leg, to end at feet clad in satin slippers. But she felt nothing remotely like a bride should on her wedding day, there was a wary resignation in the green eyes that stared back at her.

'You look beautiful,' Anne remarked. 'I can hardly wait for my wedding.'

Rose glanced at Ann. She looked as pretty as a picture wearing the same style dress in palest green. 'So do you,' Rose said softly.

Uncle Alex rapped hard on the half-open door. 'Come on, time to go.'

Ann pressed a beautiful posy of flowers into Rose's hand. 'See you at the church,' and walked off to share a car with Aunt Jean for the journey.

Alex took Rose's arm and led her out to the waiting bridal car. 'You look beautiful *lass*. Your parents would have been so proud of you today,' he murmured.

Rose felt like crying as her uncle handed her into the car and slid in beside her. Since the fatal morning when Xavier had told his father they were going to marry, and the angry ending to their picnic later the same day, she'd seen little of her prospective groom. The same night at dinner she'd sat and smiled and accepted the congratulations of everyone. The following day there had been one sticky moment when Rose and Ann were relaxing by the swimming pool. Ann had queried Rose's lightening-fast engagement. Rose had managed to persuade her cousin she'd fallen in love, and with the arrival of Jamie and Xavier at the poolside Ann had dropped the subject.

Chewing her bottom lip, Rose reflected on Xavier's behaviour that day, he'd made harmless conversation, while quite blatantly allowing his gaze to roam appreciatively over her bikini-clad form. The heat had been intense, but when Jamie had suggested they play a game of water polo in the pool Xavier had smiled grimly and flatly refused to join them.

In fact from that day Rose had barely seen Xavier alone. If she'd been harbouring a secret wish that he meant their marriage to be real it was well and truly squashed. He appeared briefly at breakfast, and then promptly disappeared. He reappeared at dinner and acted the part of the perfect host and fiancé well enough to fool everyone. Her one consolation at the predicament she found herself in was Don Pablo. His happiness was a joy to behold; it had given the old man a new lease of life.

Rose had not the heart to disillusion him; instead she'd been engulfed in a wild flurry of activity. The following weekend had been taken up without Xavier on a brief trip to England by private jet of course, returning with Ann and Jamie's parents. Teresa had taken over the organisation of the wedding. There were trips to Seville shopping, beauty parlours, the works, and even if Rose had wanted to speak to Xavier alone she never got the chance.

It didn't take a genius to work out he was avoiding her. Once the engagement had been made public he'd not so much as kissed her apart from the occasional peck on the cheek in front of the family. The conclusion was obvious; she was to be exactly what he'd stated in the beginning, a socially acceptable wife to satisfy his father. His basic masculine needs were already perfectly catered for by his mistress. Rose told herself she didn't care, and almost believed it...

Her Uncle Alex's hand squeezing hers brought her out of her reverie. They'd arrived. The church was situated at the other side of the lake in the tiny hamlet of Valdespino, the home of the workers on the ranch that was a short drive from the main house.

Too short for Rose... She felt her heart begin to pound

and if she hadn't had her uncle's arm to cling to she doubted she would make it up the few steps to the church door.

Her eyes took a moment to adjust to the dark interior of the church and when they did she caught her breath. Tall, broad-shouldered and looking incredibly handsome in an elegant pearl grey suit, Xavier was standing at the foot of the altar, watching every step she took. Her nervous gaze clashed with black eyes that suddenly blazed with a golden fire of triumphant possession that threatened to engulf her. Rose almost turned and ran...

Xavier stepped forward, and grasped her hand. She felt an inexplicable shiver race through her and froze on the spot. His dark eyes narrowed as if her hesitation angered him, and he drew her closer towards him as the priest offered a greeting and the service began.

Afterwards she remembered little of the ceremony, only the overwhelming presence of the tall brooding man by her side. The wedding ring felt like a cold hard seal of possession on her finger, and surprisingly she was given a ring to place on Xavier's finger. When the priest intoned the words, 'You may kiss the bride,' she had barely succeeded in suppressing a shudder when Xavier had taken full advantage and folded her in his arms and lowered his proud head to claim her lips with his own.

Flushed and furious, she looked up into his powerful dark face when he finally let her go, their eyes warring for a second. He didn't have to make it so convincing—a brief touch would have conformed to tradition.

'My wife,' he smiled and she trembled as he tucked her hand proprietarily under his arm and led her back down the aisle.

The mandatory photographs were taken and Rose heaved a sigh of relief as she sank gratefully into the back seat of the bridal car. A short respite before facing everyone again at the reception at the Hacienda.

'That went very well I think,' Xavier remarked sliding in beside her, his long body too close for comfort. 'And you look very beautiful my darling wife,' he opined turning towards her and trailing his glance over her slender figure with an arrogance that was as shocking as it was blatant. 'Quite virginal,' he mocked.

He knew damn fine she was no virgin, and why. 'The dress was your sister's idea, not mine,' she snapped. She must have been mad to marry the man, she thought bitterly as she met the direct gaze of his ice-black eyes. There was no tenderness in his glance, only the cold cynicism of a man studying a newly acquired possession and considering its worth. 'Personally I would have preferred black,' she said bluntly and was aware of his anger, but didn't care. She felt oddly hurt that he could make a mockery of the marriage within minutes of leaving the church. But then it was not a real marriage she firmly reminded herself.

The meal and the speeches over the Hacienda echoed with the sounds of music and laughter, the champagne flowed freely and the guests were spread out over the house and gardens. Rose smiled until her face ached, and finally she felt a blessed numbness taking over her.

Xavier's arm was firmly around her waist where it had been for most of the afternoon, he turned her fully into his arms. And lowering his head he brushed the words against her cheek. 'It's time we left for our honeymoon, Rosalyn.' His dark eyes challenged her. 'Do you want me to help you change?'

'You're joking!' And catching sight of Ann near by she added, 'That's what a bridesmaid is for!' and she grasped the girl.

While Rose was getting changed, Ann, full of enthusiasm

and quite a bit of champagne gave Rose the confirmation that Xavier had fulfilled his side of the bargain. 'Your new husband is brilliant—Jamie and I are thrilled to bits at the allowance he has arranged for us.'

'You told me, yesterday,' Rose tried to stop her. She didn't need to hear yet again how wonderful Xavier was but Ann continued to give the exact arrangement in minute detail.

Straightening the narrow straps of the designer linen sundress in a rich terra cotta, Rose picked up the matching jacket, and her purse. She'd removed the flowers from her hair, and swept it into a smooth French pleat, and felt slightly more in control. But she was almost relieved to leave. Ann's good humour was too much to bear.

Xavier was waiting for her in the hall, his frame straightening perceptibly at her approach. His dark gaze drifted down over her in an explicit sexual survey, his mobile mouth curving in a smile as he eyed the long length of her legs with obvious appreciation. It was an act for the guests, Rose told herself firmly, but it did not stop her pulse beating in her throat, and by the time she got to his side her nerves were as taut as a bow string.

'Very nice,' he murmured looping an arm around her slender shoulders and urging her across the crowded room to where his father sat surrounded by his family. Don Pablo and Teresa kissed Rose, as did Jean, Alex, Jamie and Ann. It was Ann she clung to for a moment. The young girl must never know this was all for her benefit.

The red Ferrari purred down the long drive and out onto the main road. Xavier put his foot down on the accelerator and the car surged forward in a burst of speed that threw Rose back against the seat.

'Why the rush?' she demanded.

'Hmmm,' he snorted and shot her a brief glance before returning his attention to the road. 'I'm frustrated.'

She shot him a startled glance. If he thought he was relieving his sexual frustration with her he had another think coming. 'Now wait a minute....'

'A frustrated-racing driver,' he drawled mockingly.

Embarrassed Rose closed her eyes and pretended to sleep, the effect of countless sleepless nights caught up with her and surprisingly she did.

'Rosalyn,' the husky murmur played with her dreams.

'Yes,' she sighed opening her eyes. Deep slumberous green clashed with ebony, and she couldn't prevent a swift indrawn breath. Xavier was leaning over her, his chiselled features hard as stone and something raw and savage in the depths of his eyes. His lashes drooped hiding any sign of emotion and he smiled a frightening little smile.

'We have arrived,' he said and his arm stretched across her body, his fingers unclipping her seat belt.

Rose was shaken by an awareness so intense that her hand involuntarily lifted towards his compelling face. Just in time she realised what she was doing and forced her traitorous senses back under control. She completed the gesture by running her hand over one side of her hair with what she hoped was casual ease. 'So I see.'

A man she'd never seen before appeared at the side of the car and opened the door. As she climbed out Xavier appeared at her side and made the introduction.

'Rosalyn, this is Franco—my, how do you say, Butler?'

Intrigued Rose asked, 'Then what is Max?'

'Max and Marta are my father's constant attendants. Where he goes, they go. Franco is in charge of this house; he was on holiday when you were here last.'

Walking across the massive elegant hall with Xavier a

step ahead of her and Franco leading the way carrying her suitcase, Rose had the irrepressible urge to giggle.

Marching in a single file across the vast expanse of mosaic flooring she was reminded of a comic filmstrip of the three Egyptians. She bit down hard on her bottom lip to stop the laughter breaking forth. For a couple on their wedding night it was so formal it was ridiculous.

'Something amusing you?' Xavier asked, halting and taking her arm and forcing her to face him. His touch burned like fire and she glanced at his long tanned fingers against her skin, and all amusement vanished.

She lifted her eyes to his, and saw the dangerous challenge in his smile. 'No, no nothing at all.' Where was the humour in a loveless marriage? 'But I could use a drink.' This from a girl who hardly ever drank said something for the nervous tension consuming her.

He raised his brows his eyes resting thoughtfully on her taut face. 'I think we both could. Franco has provided a cold meal in the dining room, and the champagne is on ice. Shall we?'

It was polite and civilised. Rose ate a few mouthfuls of cold meat but she couldn't have said what it was, forcing the food down a dry throat. She sipped very sparingly at a glass of champagne, determined to keep her wits about her, and all the time she felt the tension building to stifling proportions.

They exchanged meaningless platitudes. The wedding had gone well. Teresa looked well. The weather had been brilliant. Rose tried to keep up a polite conversation but Xavier's replies became more and more monosyllabic making it obvious he had no desire to comply with the social niceties. Instead he sat in a brooding silence that completely unnerved Rose, until she finally pushed back her chair and got to her feet.

'Going somewhere?' His brilliant dark gaze narrowed on her face and he stared at her for long tense seconds. The line of his jaw was taut, then he picked up his wineglass and casually took a drink as though he could not give a damn...

Rose stiffened. 'I've had enough,' and she was not just talking about the food. It was obvious the wedding was over, mission accomplished as far as Xavier was concerned. What more was there to say? 'I thought I might unpack; it's been a long day and I'm rather tired.'

'As you please,' he said smoothly. 'I believe Franco has put you in your old room.'

So that was it... He couldn't have made it plainer if he'd written it in to the marriage contract. 'Goodnight,' Rose intoned flatly and walked out of the room. Xavier did not try to stop her.

She climbed into the big gold canopied bed, some half an hour later having showered and donned the only nightie she could find, a confection in satin and lace—obviously Ann's choice. As wedding nights go she thought dryly, it was a bit of a let-down. Lying on her back she watched the silver rays of the moon shimmer and move across the ceiling. It was too hot for a cover, but out of habit she pulled the sheet up to her neck and closed her eyes.

Soon she was drifting in a kind of stupor, half asleep and half wakening. The gossamer light brush of sensuous lips against her mouth, the wonderful sensation of being enfolded in a warm protective cocoon made her sigh with pleasure. She wriggled into the heated warmth, her tongue slipping out to taste the shape and texture of the intriguing lips. Languorously she opened her eyes but saw nothing, the blackness was complete. She was dreaming. Lifting her slender arms she reached for her phantom lover, her hands curving around a hard male back, her fingers stroking over the soft silk of... She froze...

Her eyes adjusting to the darkness, she realised the dark shape was all too real. 'Xavier.' He was wearing pyjamas...

'Who else, my lovely Rosalyn.' The fiery glint in his black eyes was all too discernible. As was the hard tension of his body arching over her.

The arms that had been reaching for him instinctively tried to push him away, one hand tangling in the open pyjama jacket the other spreading over his naked hair-roughened chest. His skin felt like fire, and with remarkable ease he captured her hands in his, his body crushing hers.

'Yes, my wife,' he grated.

'What do you think you are doing?' Rose demanded in a voice that lacked conviction even to her own ears. But in the inky blackness with the scent and weight and feel of his magnificent body overpowering her she was once again plunged into the spell of his dark male sorcery, as she had been years ago.

A husky chuckle and hard warm lips covering hers was her answer.

Rose tried. She did try to resist... Closing her eyes, she willed herself to feel no emotion, but with her eyes shut it only strengthened all her other senses. She opened her mouth to deny him, and taking the advantage she so carelessly offered, his tongue sought the heated warmth of her mouth. She felt the heavy beat of his heart against her chest, the heat and rigid power of his arousal against her thigh and the devastating sensuality of his hungry lips made her senses whirl. His touch instigated an answering hunger within her that she was powerless to deny, her tongue slipping into his mouth to duel with his in a hot moist passionate kiss.

Xavier's lips finally left hers to seek the slender curve

of her throat while his free hand swept down over the satin covering her breast, taking the fabric with it. His mouth lingered on the pulse beating wildly in her neck as his hand found the creamy smoothness of her breast, the tender peak swelling with pulsing desire. She groaned a low guttural sound, as he discovered its twin and rolled the hardening peak between thumb and finger. A multitude of exquisite sensations exploded inside her, she flexed her wrists aching to touch him, to make him feel a fraction of what she felt.

His grip tightened. 'Rosalyn,' he rasped lifting his head, his black eyes gleaming down into hers. 'This is the way it has to be the first time.' With ruthless efficiency he ripped the nightgown from her body the shoulder straps giving way with a single tug from his hand.

Her heart bounded in her ears and she silently cursed the darkness that prevented her seeing his magnificent body clearly, even as her mind told her she should demand he stop.

'¡Dios! I have dreamed of this.' His huskily voiced words feathered over the soft curve of her cheek. His sensuous lips bit gently on her own, and his hand caressed a feather-light pattern down over her breasts, and lower his fingers splaying out over her stomach.

Rose was caught up in a desire so intense nothing else mattered. Her tongue greedily sought his, and when he broke the kiss, for a second she felt bereft. But then he lowered his mouth to her breasts to taste and tease each straining peak.

Her whole body seemed to pulsate with fiery pleasure, as sensation after sensation washed over her, his hand slid lower, the heel of his palm pressing on the soft curling hairs at the apex of her thighs, as his long fingers discovered the hot damp core of her.

Her body arched involuntarily to his caressing touch as

he explored every inch of her with hand and mouth in a shockingly sensual intimacy. She threw her head back, her wrist straining in his pinioning hand as great shudders of shattering sensual delight crashed through her in wave after wave. She cried out and his mouth stifled the cry, as his hand curved under her bottom, and lifted her to take the penetrating thrust of his manhood.

'Xavier.' His name escaped on a groan as he held her motionless, then slowly he began to move, filling her body, as he filled her heart and mind. A deep throbbing ache built and built until she thought she could stand no more, and then she was caught up in the pounding rhythmic passion of his total possession, and she cried out his name as they reached the savagely wild all-consuming climax together.

It was some time before she was aware of her surroundings, her naked body held beneath the heavy weight of his strong masculine frame, the steady thud of his heart against her breast and the rasp of his breathing the only sound in the darkened room. What had she done? Keeled over like a stupid teenager at his first kiss, she castigated herself.

'My sweet sensuous Rosalyn, you have not changed,' Xavier mocked huskily, as he nuzzled into the curve of her throat, and finally he let her go.

Flexing her fingers, she lowered her hands to his shoulders, intending to push him away. Deeply ashamed at her helpless surrender to him, and it seemed somehow worse when she realised, he was still wearing a pyjama jacket!

# CHAPTER NINE

ROSE LET HER ARMS FALL to her sides, her hands were free, but she knew now her body would never be free of its slavish desire for Xavier. She refused to call it love. When Xavier finally rolled away from her she lay for a long time staring into the darkness, consumed with shame at how easily he'd made her frighteningly aware of her own sensuality yet again.

'You're remarkably quiet Rosalyn,' Xavier's husky comment broke the silence. He turned on his side, his shadowed outline looming over her, a glint of pure male satisfaction in his eyes. One long finger traced the bow of her lips. 'You surprised me, you were so hungry for it. If I didn't know better I'd say it was some considerable time since you had sex.'

From the dizzy heights of ecstasy to brutal reality, Rose did the only thing she could. She hid her shattered emotions beneath a cool sophistication. 'What is there to say. You're a great lover, but then hundreds of women must have told you so, after all you've had plenty of practice,' she opined sarcastically. 'Pity you're not so hot on keeping a promise.'

'You're straying into dangerous territory,' Xavier said coldly 'I have not forgotten or forgiven the way you ran out on me after our first liaison.'

Her attempt at sophistication vanished at his hurtful reminder. 'Neither have I, nor have I forgotten how you blackmailed me into this marriage with the promise it would be platonic,' she hissed at him, all the anger and humiliation she'd suffered at his hands rising like bile in her throat. 'You're a lying swine and I hate you.'

'I never promised a platonic marriage; you heard what you wanted to hear,' he retaliated curtly. 'As for hate. I'd have it any day to false avowals of love. Your hate makes you melt in my arms, and cry out for my possession. You tell me who is the bigger liar?'

Something in his eyes made her shiver and she shoved hard at his chest. But he merely laughed a harsh cruel sound and then he lowered his head to her breast. Finding the soft tip, with unerring accuracy and licking it with his tongue before taking it into his mouth.

'No, no...' Rose cried, her hands reaching for his head and tangling in the thickness of his hair as she tried to pull him away.

'Is it hate that makes your breast swell to my touch?' he asked mockingly, while his hand moved in a sensual caress down her naked length. He raised his head and the brilliant blaze of his eyes scorched into hers, as he claimed her mouth with a searing passion that seemed to burn to her soul.

Despite her best effort to deny him, she could not prevent the shudder of pleasure that betrayed her. Her hands found the opening of his pyjama jacket and moved hungrily across the warm, hair-roughened chest towards the broad shoulders, where the hard muscles rippled beneath her caressing fingers. And she didn't care that her capitulation proved how humiliatingly easily he could arouse her, because he groaned against her mouth, his body hard and tense with an urgency he could not hide, and she realised it was the same for him as she slipped the jacket from his shoulders.

They made love in a wild fury of passion. Xavier grasped her hands and dragged them low down over his firm buttocks, and she explored the smooth male flesh, trailing her fingers over the hard sweep of muscle from hip to thigh, and 'round to the rigid heat of his manhood.

'¡Dios sí,' he groaned as she caressed the long length of him with tactile delight. 'Ah! Rosalyn what you do to me,' he rasped and tearing her hands from his body he turned her beneath him and thrust into the silken centre of her. The pounding rhythm of his great body driving her to new heights of exquisite pleasure that left her totally exhausted and utterly fulfilled.

Xavier pulled her into the hard curve of his side. He reached to push back the damp strands of hair from her brow then nuzzling her ear husked something in Spanish. Rose sighed and turned fully into his arms, burying her head against his broad chest where she could hear the throbbing rhythmic beat of his heart and there she slept.

When Rose awoke, she was completely disorientated. The room was still dark, and the weight of a man's arm was flung across her stomach. Realisation dawned and with it came the shameful knowledge of how easy she'd fallen into Xavier's arms again. She stretched and flexed her limbs aching in places she had never ached before, and tried to ease out from beneath his restraining arm.

Xavier muttered something in his sleep but he didn't wake up. He stirred restlessly and rolled over onto his back and she was free. She slipped along the bed, and froze as someone knocked on the door, calling Xavier's name.

The door opened sending a swathe of light across the room quickly followed by the light being switched on and the smiling figure of Franco walking sedately towards the bed carrying a coffee tray.

Three things happened at once. Rose lay back and made a grab for the sheet to cover herself, suddenly realising she was naked. Xavier opened his eyes and sat up in bed. 'What the hell?' and Rose glancing up was presented with the sight of his broad back.

'Oh, my God!' Flowing like a river from under his arm a massive scar flooded down the side of his once beautifully bronzed body to cover half of his back 'What happened to you?' she asked unevenly. It didn't take a doctor to see he'd been very badly burned at some time. Some attempt had been made at plastic surgery but the scarring was unmistakable. The agony it must have caused him made her want to weep.

Xavier's voice cracked out, sharp as a whip. 'Get out Franco.' And not waiting to see he was obeyed Xavier turned his head and stared down at where she lay. She'd no idea how beautiful she looked, with a cloud of red hair laced through with gold shimmering across the pillow, her wide mouth swollen with his kisses, and her green eyes warm and compassionate on his handsome face. But he did not want her pity, it was too little, too late.

'What did you expect from a car crash? A neat little scar?' He drawled cynically. 'You're a doctor, surely you can recognise the effect of burning oil.'

Wriggling up into a sitting position, she impulsively reached out her hand to his back, her slender fingers tracing over the puckered flesh. 'I never knew, I'm sorry,' she offered quietly. Suddenly a lot of little things made sense. His refusal to join them all in the pool at the Hacienda. Last night she'd gone to bed with moonlight shining in the window. Xavier must have closed the heavy drapes blocking out any light before joining her in bed. The Pyjamas!

His gaze lanced through her. 'You knew all right.' Shrugging off her hand he was out of the bed, totally unconcerned by his naked state, his eyes glittering hard as they flicked over her. 'You have the face of an angel and you lie like the devil.'

Rose was horrified by his revelation and confused. It was not the first time he'd called her a liar, but why she had no idea, and she stared at him silently, her eyes wide and tinged with a puzzled compassion. Perhaps his accident had been in the newspapers, and he assumed everyone knew. In her capacity as a doctor she was aware it was not unusual for someone who had suffered a serious accident to be a little paranoid about it.

'I don't need or want your sympathy,' Xavier declared harshly, glimpsing the compassion in her gaze and angered by it. 'Your body is all I want, and as I proved quite spectacularly last night you wanted mine, so don't bother denying it.'

Incredible as it was to believe Rose realised Xavier, her powerful arrogant husband, was vulnerable in one respect. He'd deliberately kept his body hidden from her eyes, and recalling their lovemaking, he had even skilfully manoeuvred her hands so she had touched just about everywhere else but his back.

What had happened? No, she amended, *who* had been cruel enough to reject him because of his scars, his dead wife maybe? Rose didn't know but her heart bled for him, and she felt like strangling the person who had been so insensitive. It was in that moment that she realised that she loved him, probably always had.

Her hand tightened on the sheet. Loved him hopelessly for the rest of her life, probably for all eternity. Emotion choked her and she swallowed hard lowering her lashes to mask her expression from him. 'I wasn't going to,' she finally responded feeling her way.

His mouth curved in a cynical twist. 'Though you would rather not have to look at me. But no matter, you know what they say—all cats are grey in the night.'

Rose was appalled when she heard what he said, and

forgetting she was naked she sprang out of bed and stood barely a foot away from him. 'That's a horrible thing to say. I...' She bit down hard on her bottom lip horrified she had almost confessed she loved him... Wary green eyes flew to his face, and she blushed scarlet.

He was studying her nude body with obvious appreciation, his brows drawing together in a faint frown, at the few darkening bruises on the soft flesh of her uptilted breasts. 'Did I hurt you?' he asked huskily.

She wanted to say yes, a strange mixture of love and resentment stirring in her, but she could not lie to him. 'No,' she murmured, a certain pride in her body and his obvious delight in it caused her to stand a little straighter.

'Good,' he murmured but he had already forgotten the question as he glanced lower to the apex of her thighs, and on down the long length of her legs.

Rose in her turn could not resist appreciating his body, the scar from his face angled down over one shoulder and under his arm but she barely registered it. His chest was broad, liberally covered with black curling hairs that arrowed down past a narrow waist and taut lean hips. Long muscular legs flexed.

Her whole body blushed when she saw the very masculine reaction to her blatant scrutiny of his naked state, and her confidence deserted her. 'I need a shower,' and spinning on her heel she fled into the bathroom, his husky chuckle following her.

Pulling on white lace briefs, she'd taken from one of the drawers in the dressing room, she deftly slipped on the matching bra. Someone had unpacked her clothes, probably one of the maids she mused. Showered and almost dressed she felt more in control of her wayward emotions. Opening a wardrobe door she withdrew a hanger holding a green cotton dress. In seconds she'd pulled it over her head, and smoothed the skirt down over her hips. She could hear water running; and, realising she must have left a tap on, she walked back through into the bathroom and stopped. Through the glass of the shower door was the unmistakable figure of Xavier, water cascading down over his magnificent body, his proud head thrown back, his eyes closed.

She was staring again! She blinked and hastily shot back into the bedroom, her glance dropping to the rumpled bed and quickly away again. She did not need to be reminded it was the scene of her downfall. Spying the coffee Franco had provided, she poured herself a cup. She crossed to the window and flung back the heavy drapes. It was another brilliant sunny day, but her thoughts were anything but sunny. Sipping the coffee she grimaced in distaste; it was almost cold, but she needed the jolt of caffeine to try and bring some order to her befuddled brain. Draining the cup, she spun around. She had to get out of here, but halfway across the room she stopped, her head lifting sharply as Xavier strolled out of the bathroom.

His black hair was plastered to his head, and he was naked apart from a towel slung low around his hips. She gulped. 'Bad enough you invade my bedroom but at least you could use your own bathroom,' she snapped. Only then did she notice the clothes he was carrying.

He frowned at her. '*That is* our bathroom.' He dropped the clothes on the rumpled bed.

'Just a minute, you said this was my bedroom.' After her sojourn in the shower and some heavy thinking Rose had acknowledged that much as she loved Xavier, it did not make their marriage any better. He was still a devious devil, he had a mistress but it did not stop him climbing into Rose's bed, plus ten years ago he had used her quite abominably, however much he tried to pretend to the contrary. He'd married his fiancée, proof enough for any woman that he'd used her and Rose was not an idiot. She loved him but she was not going to be any man's doormat. She had too much pride, she deserved better.

He paused in the process of unfolding a pair of boxer shorts. 'This gold room *is* the master suite Rosalyn,' he said with sardonic humour. He then proceeded to drop the towel from his hips and step into the navy silk shorts.

'But the first night I was here you told me it was a guest bedroom.' Her eyes flashed angrily, their gleaming jade depths reflecting her inner turmoil.

'But nothing Rosalyn. It pleased me to have you in here from the day you arrived, because I had every intention of marrying you.'

His deep lazy drawl sent an icy chill feathering across the surface of her skin. To guess he had plotted to get her to Spain was bad enough, to have him confirm it was chilling. Her startled gaze locked with his.

'I vowed ten years ago that vengeance would be mine, and one day, I would have you again. You dropped out of sight, but from the minute I saw you step out of your E-Type Jaguar at Teresa's your fate was sealed.' And with a shrug of his broad shoulders he added, 'And I succeeded, *querida;* easier than I could have hoped.' He gave her a chilling smile, the endearment said in mockery.

For a long moment his confession left her totally speechless, he'd married her for some twisted revenge... Rose couldn't believe it. If any one had just cause for revenge it was her not him! She wanted to knock the sardonic smile of his face; instead she fought for control and won. 'But why?' she demanded, she needed to know. 'What did I ever do to hurt you?'

'Oh, you didn't hurt me. As I recall your last words ten years ago were *"I don't need the key or you. Goodbye,"* and hung up on...'

'And that's *it?*' she interrupted incredulously. 'Because I dumped you?' Anger made her voice rise an octave. He'd turned her life upside down simply because she'd dented his colossal pride by hanging up on him. The chauvinistic pig was used to women hanging on to his every word, and did not appreciate being jilted. What blasted arrogance! She fumed, 'Or maybe you expected more for the price of a dress?' she raged. Obviously he had not thought he had got his money's worth from one night. 'You're despicable.'

'Maybe.' His eyes flared and his facial muscles tightened into a mask of controlled anger. 'But you're here and you're my wife. Tradition was upheld, virtually every Valdespino bride has spent her wedding night in the harem bed,' he gestured to the bed with a nod of his dark head. 'It's considered to be a fertility symbol. Though in your case it probably does not apply. Protection against pregnancy must be a way of life for you.'

She opened her mouth to deny his claim and closed it. His scathing comment reminded her of her own pregnancy and the tragic outcome. Pain knotted her stomach as though a knife was being twisted in her gut. How could she love this man? She'd actually thought he was vulnerable, but he didn't care a jot about her. For a man who'd gone to great lengths to hide his body from her twenty-four hours ago, he'd certainly had a swift change of heart, she thought bitterly. If it was possible he appeared even more handsome wearing only boxer shorts, his intensely masculine frame exuding an innate sexuality that was lethal in its potency. He was so damnably attractive a million scars could never obliterate the virile power of the man. She watched him pick up a pair of beige chinos from where he'd left them on the bed, step into them, and pull the zip. Then he slipped on a short-sleeved white shirt, fasten the buttons, and tucked the tail into his trousers, before clasping the buckle of a sleek hide belt at his waist.

'Have you finished?'

She was suddenly conscious she had been staring again. 'No I have not.' Her chin took on a defensive tilt, and she held his knowing gaze. 'And as for you and your hide-bound traditions, they certainly didn't do your first wife much good, because you don't have any children.' Reminded of his betrayal she lashed out at him any way she could. 'Or should I say none that are legitimate.' The memory of his mistresses adding to her hurt anger.

In two lithe strides he was beside her. She was tempted to move back a few steps, shivering at the ice-cold eyes boring into hers, but she refused to give in to the feeling of intimidation that his large body towering over her provoked.

'You did not know my late wife, and you will not mention her again.' His hard dark face was expressionless, but only a fool would fail to detect the steel beneath silky smoothness of his voice. 'Understand?'

Rose was beginning to. His sainted wife was loved, and yet it hadn't stopped him betraying the poor girl with Rose all those years ago, and suddenly all the fury, the resentment, the hurt she'd been harbouring for years overflowed.

'Oh! I understand all right. The same way you never mentioned you were engaged to her ten years ago when you tricked me into bed with you. You haven't changed a bit; still the manipulative devil you always were,' she snapped furiously, only to find her shoulders gripped in fingers of steel.

'That's where you're wrong, Rosalyn. I am no longer a fool for a pretty face,' he said fixing her with a piercing glance that sent a sliver of fear down her spine. 'Nor was I betrothed to another woman when I met you. That is a pretence you've invented to salve your guilty conscious for running out on me.'

'Don't insult my intelligence,' she protested hotly. 'I saw the photograph on the mantelpiece, and Sebastian—'

'You will not mention his name in my presence.' He cut her off, and she was struck dumb by the violence in his tone. His hands bit deeper into the soft flesh of her upper arms. 'I will not have you maligning my friend to feed your guilty conscience.'

'*My* guilty conscience?' Rose exclaimed, her hands clenching at her sides.

'I've been patient with you. I have demanded no explanation for your past actions.'

Her temper flared red hot, her eyes flashing 'You've got a bloody nerve,' she swore. 'Or a damned convenient memory.'

Xavier went peculiarly white around the mouth. 'Don't drive me too far Rosalyn,' he warned savagely. 'I have kept my temper, and played the gentleman but not anymore.'

'You a gentleman, don't make me laugh,' she spat scathingly. 'You've done nothing but manipulate me and push me around from the day we met.'

'Enough,' he said, and there was something so savagely contemptuous in his expression that Rose tried to step back. Amazingly Xavier let her, his hands falling from her shoulders.

'Arguing over the past is a futile exercise, Rosalyn. You are my wife.' Then with a level look at her proud angry face he said with a return to his usual cold aloof composure. 'And as such you will endeavour to behave with suitable decorum. Swearing is out, and I am quite prepared to draw a veil over the past and call a truce.'

He sounded like he was addressing a board meeting... She opened her mouth to rage at him. She was sick of being taken for a mug by the arrogant devil, but stopped, biting down hard on her bottom lip.

He stood a foot away, the top button unfastened on his immaculate white shirt. 'I will not question you on your past lovers, Dominic and the rest, and you will grant me the same accord,' he drawled, his sensuous lips twisting in an ironic curve that did not quite make it as a smile.

Guilty colour washed over her face and she fought it back. She'd done nothing to be ashamed of. Dominic had been a kind sensitive man and a good friend. But it had not worked. He'd told her afterwards. *"You're a one-man woman and unfortunately for me I am not the lucky man."* But how had Xavier guessed about Dominic? She'd only mentioned the man once.

His astuteness was amazing, but one look at his hawkish features, the sheer steel-like strength of character the handsome face did not quite disguise, she conceded Xavier was far too astute for her to waste her time trying to defy him. Why not enjoy what he was prepared to give her without hankering for more. Last night she'd lost herself in a physical ecstasy she'd given up hope of ever experiencing again. The fact she loved him and he didn't was not that important, she'd reached the age of twenty-nine, a bit too old to wish for heart and flowers, she told herself wryly.

'By your silence I take it you agree,' Xavier prompted with a sardonic arch of one dark brow. 'Face it Rosalyn we are both mature enough to realise the futility of such confessions. You have an English phrase, no? "It is water under the bridge." Agreed?'

'Agreed,' Rose said quietly, 'But with one proviso.' She lifted fearless green eyes to his. 'I demand absolute fidelity from you.' He didn't love her but given time he might learn to, but not if she had to share him with his mistress. She was not a complete fool...

She'd surprised him. His expression flared with some brilliant emotion, and he took a step towards her. 'But of course you have my word, *querida*,' Xavier drawled, a gleam of humour in his dark eyes. 'But understand I demand no less from you.' His hand reached out to her and she took a swift step back.

'Wait. Haven't you forgotten something?' Rose said curtly 'Or should I say someone.' She watched as his dark eyes drew together in a puzzled frown. 'The mistress you mentioned when you so eloquently proposed to me,' she reminded him sarcastically.

Xavier grimaced. 'I am almost forty, and I've been alone for some years. It would be foolish to deny I have kept a mistress in the past, but not now. Last night with you was the first time I had made love to a woman in six months or more.' And before she guessed his intent his hand curved around her nape, and his mouth covered hers in a long hard kiss, her belated attempt to break free was useless as his other arm circled her waist and drew her close in against him. When he finally lifted his head her eyes were filled with anger and pain.

'This isn't going to work, Xavier,' she told him bluntly. 'I will not live with a liar.'

'Are you referring to me?' he asked incredulously, tension sizzling in the air as they faced each. 'Nobody, but nobody has ever doubted my word. How you...'

'Stop.' Rose held up her hand palm to his face. 'Dinner, the first night in Seville, a telephone call. Jogging your memory?' she prompted sarcastically.

Without comment Xavier strolled towards the door, and Rose's gaze followed him taking in the tense set of his wide shoulders. He spun on his heel, and she noted the flush of guilty colour emphasising his high cheekbones. 'Who told you? Not my father.'

'Jamie joked about it after your father retired for the night.'

'He would!' he opined in a flat chilling voice coming to stand in front of her. 'But he obviously did not give you the whole story.' Rose wasn't sure she wanted to hear it anymore and she tried desperately to mask her confused feelings looking somewhere over his shoulder as he continued. 'I am not in the habit of explaining my actions to anyone, least of all a woman.'

Bravely she raised her eyes to his and said bluntly, 'I'm not any woman, I am your wife.'

His eyes rested almost thoughtfully on her taut face. 'Yes, you are right.' His lashes drooped, hiding any sign of emotion in his dark eyes. 'Cast your mind back, Rosalyn. There was a telephone call for me at dinner, and my father was furious *before* I answered it. He was furious because the lady in question had telephoned here quite a few times over the last few months, and also while I was in England. As my father succinctly pointed out, a good mistress should be seen occasionally but not heard, and certainly not in one's own home.'

'My God, that is archaic!' Rose exclaimed in disgust.

'Maybe but true. I took the telephone call, and decided to put an end to it immediately. After all I had you.'

His supreme arrogance took her breath away. 'What did you do—pay her off?'

'Something like that, suffice it to say it is over, finished, and the lady in question was very satisfied.'

Rose's eyebrows drew together in a quick frown he must have slept with her for the last time.

'In the monetary sense, not the sexual,' Xavier drawled mockingly, accurately reading her mind 'You have no reason to doubt my word or my fidelity.' A dangerous smile curved his hard mouth, his hand reaching out to trace the line of her jaw before, bending down his lips covering hers in a gentle strangely evocative kiss.

She could believe him, or not as she wished, and with the taste of him on her mouth, she was so intensely aware of him. It was no contest.

'Make up your mind, Rosalyn,' he prompted huskily. 'Because it is almost noon and I am dying of hunger.'

Involuntarily her glance flicked to the bed and back to his face.

'That as well.' One dark brow arched eloquently. 'But right now for food.' And at that precise moment a distinct grumbling noise came from his stomach. He grinned slightly shamefacedly. 'I was so nervous yesterday I hardly ate a thing all day.'

His confession made him seem so much more human, and she grinned back. 'Let's eat.'

'Can you cook?' Xavier asked, preceding her to the door and holding it open.

'What if I say, "no"? Is it grounds for a divorce?' she questioned snaking past him, with a provocative toss of her head, suddenly feeling light-hearted for the first time in weeks.

Just as suddenly a large arm slipped around her waist halting her progress along the hall. 'No, Rosalyn. There will be no divorce.' Xavier held her still his eyes watchful and incredibly dark 'Ever. I want you to be the mother of my children.'

Her heart missed a beat. Had he guessed she was pregnant when she had tried to contact him? Could he really be so cruelly insensitive? Her eyes were wide, unblinking as she searched his features for a visible sign that would give her an answer, but there was none.

'Think about it.' Xavier reached out and pushed a stray tendril of hair back behind her ear, his lips curling in a slow wry smile. 'As for the cooking. I will do it. Franco always goes to eleven o'clock mass on Sunday and has the rest of the day off.'

'Ah, now I understand, you expect me to slave over a hot stove,' she teased, while wryly acknowledging it was the easier option. Much as she loved him there would always be a barrier between the two of them. Some subjects and people were not open for discussion.

# CHAPTER TEN

BREAKFAST. Brunch. Whatever…was a convivial meal. Much to Rose's astonishment the kitchen was large and very modern, not the least in keeping with the rest of the house, and just as he had been on their very first night together Xavier was a very good cook.

'The ham and scrambled egg were perfect,' she offered, forking the last few crumbs into her mouth, and glancing across the width of the stainless-steel table, to where Xavier was sitting watching her obvious delight with some satisfaction.

'Then let me surprise you again. Go and grab your bag and a bikini and we will go away for a few days.'

'Away! Where?' she asked, astonishment widening her green eyes.

'I have a villa in Marbella. It's little more than a couple of hours away by car, and on the coast it will be a degree or two cooler than here.'

'But why? We only arrived last night, and Franco has just unpacked all my clothes. It will take me ages to pack again.'

Dark brown eyes gleaming with amusement met hers. 'Really Rosalyn, one can buy anything in Marbella; it is the jet-set capital of Europe.' One eyebrow slanted mockingly. 'Unless of course you want me to come upstairs and help you, but I have a feeling it might delay our departure indefinitely.'

He looked a very civilised, sophisticated man Rose thought as her breasts pushed against the confines of her bra in tingling awareness. He was obviously quite used to exchanging sensual innuendoes over the breakfast table with the current lady in his life. She wondered if he knew how tempting his casual sexual offer sounded to her.

'Decision time, Rosalyn.'

The sound of his faintly teasing drawl jolted her into action. She pushed back her chair and stood up. 'Give me ten minutes.'

The villa was built on a terrace into the hillside high above Marbella and to Rose's surprise it was quite new. Approached by a tree-lined steep winding drive, it seemed to be perched on a ledge of the cliff.

'This is fantastic,' Rose said sliding out of the car and glancing around. There was no garden as such. Xavier had parked the car in front of a garage door underneath the main building. Wide wooden steps led up to a thirty-foot-wide deck that surrounded three sides of the house, with enormous long supports sunk forty feet or so down the hill. 'Dangerous but fantastic,' she added as Xavier moved to her side carrying the little luggage they'd brought in one hand.

'Life is dangerous. We take what we can when we can,' Xavier opined cynically, his dark eyes skimming over with brooding intensity.

Now what had she done, she wondered following his long-legged figure through the door into a cool tiled foyer.

Two doors opened off the hall. Xavier flung one open and remarked, 'The kitchen,' and then strode past her to disappear through the other one.

Once more she trailed after him. This was becoming a habit, she thought dryly, eyeing the taut line of his wide shoulders, as he swept across the vast expanse of the room to a door at the far side.

Deliberately she stopped and looked around, her mouth

falling open in stunned amazement. A wall of glass opened out onto the deck, and the view was unbelievable. She slid open the glass doors and stepped outside. What feat of engineering had made it possible she did not know, but there was a rectangular swimming pool, and a couple of meters away a hot tub. She crossed to the far side of the deck and leaned her arms against the protective rail and stared... The panoramic view captured and held the eye. The gleaming white buildings of Marbella, the enormous marina and then the clear blue of the sea stretching to the distant horizon.

'A bustling town is not perhaps the first choice for a honeymoon,' Xavier's deep voice was behind her and she spun around. 'But with my father's health, or lack of it, I should say, I do not want to leave the country at present.'

'I understand,' she murmured, her gaze meshed with his, and suddenly the rail behind her seemed too fragile. His dark saturnine features swam before her eyes. He was like some dark avenging eagle and this house was his eyrie and she was trapped. She felt dizzy, she stepped towards him, and his arms curved around her.

'What is it?' he asked his dark brows drawing together in a frown. 'Rosalyn?'

Shaking her head to dispel the image, she forced a smile to her lips. 'Nothing; just the heat. I think I will have a swim.'

'Good idea. I have a few calls to make and then I might join you.'

There was only the one bedroom, a vast room that opened off a small internal hall from the living room. The same wall of glass and the same view, but with a luxurious *en suite*. Quickly she stripped off her clothes and pulled on a black bikini. Swiftly twisting her hair into a long plait she opened the glass door and walked back out onto the deck. Xavier had gone.

She slid into the pool, the cool water soothing her over-heated flesh. The trouble was she thought sadly, she was always overheating around her powerful husband irrespective of the temperature, and she did not know what to do about it. She forged through the water length after length and tried to make some sense of her confused thoughts. She knew her own nature far too well. Whatever she did, she always did with one hundred percent commitment. As a model she was the best she could be. With medicine she made exactly the same total commitment. Floating over onto her back she remembered her boss's words when he told her to go home and rest. *'Your parents were a wonderful couple and always responded to an emergency anywhere in the world when requested but they had you and each other, a family. You are an intelligent, beautiful woman and a good doctor, always concerned for the less fortunate in the world, but you are always alone. It is time you considered your own needs, perhaps even make a home of your own.'*

Rose closed her eyes, her arms spread wide in the water, flicking her fingers occasionally to keep afloat. She was married to the man she loved. She could already be pregnant. Did it matter that Xavier had married her for some stupid notion of vengeance probably because she was the first or only woman ever to walk out on him? The male ego was a very fragile thing she mused. But he was the best, in fact the only chance she had of ever having a family of her own. He had already said divorce was not an option. What was she beating herself up over? Her complaint was emotional not practical. The reality was she was married to an extremely wealthy man, relaxing in a swimming pool in a luxury villa...

Then she was drowning... Two large hands grabbed her waist and pulled her under the water, in a tangle of arms and legs she fought her way to the surface. Blinking water out of her eyes. 'What did you do that for?' she spluttered, frantically grasping his broad shoulders to stop herself going under again.

He did not answer, his hands grasped her waist and he dragged her hard against his large body, and simply covered her mouth with his own, parting her lips with a deliberate sensuality that she instantly succumbed to and returned.

'I've been watching you for the past ten minutes, and you're driving me mad.' His lips trailed down to her throat and he sucked the fiercely pounding pulse he found there, and then he raised his head, his dark eyes dilated to black. 'I want you...now.'

With water streaming off his bronzed body he climbed out of the pool, pulling Rose by the hand after him. She did not have time to think. He spun her back into his arms, his mouth hungry on hers, his hands stripping off the two bits of cotton she wore. He shucked off his shorts and dropping to his knees he laid her down on the deck caressing with hand and mouth every curve and crevice, until she cried out her need. His black eyes shadowed with lust and hunger bored into hers as he took her mouth again and at the same time took her willing body.

It was fast and furious and totally annihilating. Rose thought she had fainted from the exquisite pleasure. Slowly she opened her eyes, and was staring up at clear blue sky, she turned her head slightly. Xavier was lying beside her flat on his stomach, shudders still moving his wide shoulders. The scarring on his back glistened in the sun, and she reached a tentative hand towards him, stroking over the jagged flesh.

'Are you all right?' she murmured breathlessly her hand

splaying over the scar as he turned on his side. His glance flicked to where her hand rested and then to her face.

'That should be my line,' he laughed without humour. 'I lost control. A first for me.' Getting to his feet he swept her up in his arms again. 'The scar does not bother you?'

'No I've seen thousands worse, but what are you doing...' she asked breathlessly

'Penance for falling on you.' Strangely he seemed shaken, and cradling her in his arms carried her into the house. Rose glanced up through the thick curl of her lashes, and saw that his expression was rueful and nowhere near as arrogant as he normally was.

'What kind of penance?' she prompted feeling oddly protected and at peace in the comfort of his arms. Then she realised they were in the bathroom.

He set her on her feet in the shower stall and stepped in with her and turned on the overhead spray. With gentle hands he washed every inch of her body, and she returned the favour. They made it to the bed, but only just...

ROSE OPENED HER EYES, it was dark, and sitting up in bed she glanced towards the window. The house was so high that from the bed the only view was the sky. It was like living in the clouds the land of the mythological Gods she thought fancifully.

'Rosalyn.' Xavier stirred beside her and abruptly sat up. 'You're still here?' His hand clasped around her forearm.

She glanced at him surprised by the roughness of his tone. 'Of course I was just thinking how peaceful and quiet it is.' She felt his grip on her arm slacken, and his warm breath tease a few stray tendrils of her hair as he curved his arm around her shoulders and pulled her back against him.

'I'm glad you approve,' Xavier murmured, his lips seeking the elegant curve of her throat. But this time it was Rose's tummy that rumbled.

'No more of that until you feed me,' she teased pushing him away.

In a remarkably short space of time they were in the car and travelling down into the town. Xavier parked the car, and taking her hand helped her out.

'It's only a short walk to the restaurant,' he offered slipping a casual arm around her shoulders, and guiding her through the throng of people.

Rose's head was spinning like a top. Marbella was a beautiful brash town heaving with tourists, all devoted to conspicuous consumption. As they strolled past the Marina Rose's eyes were out on stalks.

'My God you could pay off the debt of every Third World country with the cash that has been spent on these yachts alone,' she exclaimed glancing up at Xavier.

His eyes gleamed with amusement 'Damn!' he wiped his brow with the heel of his hand. 'I forgot your radical views on the distribution of wealth. This is the last place I should have brought you.'

'You're right there. I feel considerably under-dressed or do I mean over-dressed. I've never seen so many gorgeous girls in one place.' Her eyes followed on particular long-legged blonde wearing a pellmet for a skirt, and a bra. Xavier's husky chuckle drew her eyes back to his. 'It's not funny I only have this one frock with me.'

'Don't worry *querida*. Tomorrow we will go shopping. But we have arrived.' Dropping his arm to her waist he guided her into the restaurant.

The décor was elegant and expensive Rose noted as they were shown to their table, and it needed only a glance to realise the patrons were among the best dressed and wealthiest around; she grimaced at her own simple green shift dress.

'You are the most beautiful woman in the place,' Xavier drawled, accurately reading her thoughts. 'So relax. Shall I order for you?'

'Yes, please.' She gave him a grateful smile for the compliment, and decided to enjoy what was on offer. The food was perfect, the wine chilled and by the time they reached the coffee stage Rose was feeling mellow and completely relaxed. Then a stunning petite dark-haired beauty stopped at their table and spoke in Spanish to Xavier for a good five minutes.

The woman's flawless figure was encased in a red satin designer gown. Diamonds sparkled at her throat and ears, but the smile she turned on Xavier just before she left, outshone them all. Rose felt a familiar stab of pain in the region of her stomach. She was no competition against the glamorous sophisticates in her husband's life. Basically she did not want to be, she recognised with a pensive smile.

'What are you thinking?' Xavier demanded.

Rose cast him a startled glance. 'I was wondering who your lady friend was. You never introduced me.'

'Isabelle is not my friend, she was a friend of my late wife.' Rose's eyes searched his dark face quizzically. It was an odd thing to say; surely any friend of his wife's would also be his. 'So tell me Rosalyn, when did you decide to become a doctor and go to medical school?'

It was such an abrupt change of subject Rose answered without thinking. 'My parents were doctors and I always intended to follow in their foot steps. I started university the September I was nine...nineteen.' She hesitated, the past was a taboo subject...

But his voice was level and light, totally at odds with the anger she could see in his eyes. 'So when we first met you knew you were going to university in the autumn, you had no intention of continuing as a model.'

'No... I mean, yes.' He smiled and it made her nervous. 'Yes, I knew I was going to university, I took a gap year to model. But I thought we were not supposed to mention the past—your instruction.'

Xavier got to his feet, threw some money on the table, and taking her hand helped her to her feet. 'You're right but I was curious. Forget it and let's go.'

After five days of sun, sea and sex, Rose stood in front of the mirror, and put the finishing touches to her make-up. A quick flick of a mascara brush and the subtle look she had been seeking was achieved. She slipped into the exquisite black designer dress, one of the many items of clothing Xavier had insisted she purchase over the past few days, and did a twirl. A fine halter strap supported the low-cut, softly draped neckline, cut away to dip to her waist at the back, the long skirt skimming her slim hips to taper down to floor length, the black gossamer knit fabric high-lighted with a subtle weaving of satin threads. Matching black high-heeled sandals completed the outfit, and she stood back from the mirror very satisfied with her sophis-ticated image, and walked out onto the deck.

'You're ready,' Xavier drawled, leaning against the safety rail his firm lips curved in a smile.

'Yes.' Her eyes swept over his tall lithe frame, her heart jolting. He looked devastatingly attractive clad in an im-maculately tailored dinner suit.

'You look good enough to eat,' he murmured, his dark eyes appraising the elegant picture she presented, and moved towards her.

'Not on your life,' she held up a defensive hand guessing his intention by the deepening gleam in his dark eyes. 'It has taken me ages to get ready, you're not mussing me up again.'

Xavier chuckled. 'You have a one-track mind, wife. I only wanted to give you this,' and from his jacket pocket he withdrew a velvet box and opening it he took out the most magnificent diamond and emerald necklace Rose had ever seen. Stepping behind her he fixed the shimmering jewels around her neck.

The movement of her hand was involuntary as she reached up and trailed her fingers over the cold stones. 'For me?' she murmured, seeing her reflection in the glass door. With her long hair swept up in curls on the top of her head, the necklace was revealed in all its glory. Her eyes flew to Xavier's. 'It is beautiful. But it must have cost a fortune.'

A faint smile tugged at the corners of his mouth. 'And you are beautiful, too, Rosalyn, and it is a wedding present so please, no dissertation on world poverty. We have not got time.'

The party was being held in a private villa by one of the wealthiest customers of the Valdespino bank. Once it had got around that Xavier was in town there had been dozens of invitations, verbal and written. But tonight was the only one he'd accepted, and tomorrow they were returning to the Hacienda.

It was an elegant affair, with about a hundred guests invited to share a buffet meal, and dance. Rose soon realised she was the talking point of the evening, the great Xavier Valdespino's new wife. She said as much to him when after supper he took her in his arms and held fast against his strong body they moved in perfect unison around the dance floor.

Xavier's dark eyes gleamed down into hers, 'It's not the fact you are my wife, but the fact you are the most beautiful, sexiest lady here. The women are green with envy and the men want to bed you,' he drawled with dry cynicism. His hand snaked up her spine and hugged her for a second as the music stopped playing.

The host of the party, a squat dark-headed man in his sixties, approached with his wife, and spoke to Xavier. Then in heavily accented English, he asked, 'Do you mind Rosalyn? I have need to steal your husband for a moment, my wife will accompany you.'

She smiled her agreement glancing up at Xavier. 'Business before pleasure, hmm?'

'Not for long I assure you,' he responded huskily, the sensual promise in those dark eyes was impossible to miss, and she watched him stroll off with the ghost of a smile playing around her lips.

Their marriage was going better than she could have ever hoped a week ago, a contented sigh escaped. The cold aloof Xavier that had insisted she marry him had given way to a warm humorous, sexy man. He might not love her yet, but she was pretty sure it would not be long before he did.

The poor hostess tried to make conversation with Rose but as neither of them spoke each other's language it was heavy going until some one else caught the hostess's attention. Rose heaved a sigh of relief and slipped quietly into the crowd.

'Well, if it isn't Xavier's new wife.' Rose spun 'round quickly, her glance colliding with the bitter brown eyes of Isabelle, the woman from the restaurant.

'Good evening,' Rose said politely.

'Not very good for you—Xavier has deserted you already? Get used to it he does that with all his women.' The malice in the other woman's eyes made Rose cringe, and backing away, she bumped into someone.

Grateful for the excuse she turned around and said, 'I am terribly sorry.'

The man was shorter than her, but attractive with laughter gleaming in his eyes. 'Don't apologise, dance with me.'

She was about to refuse when she recognised him. 'Sebastian.'

'Yes,' and wrapping his arm around her waist he led her into the crowd of dancers. 'It pains my Spanish soul to admit, lovely lady, that I do not remember your name.'

A gleam of mischief sparked in Rose's eyes. He did not recognise her. 'Rosalyn. Doctor Rosalyn May.'

'Ah yes! I remember you now, how could I have forgotten?' His hand tightened on her waist as they executed a swift turn. 'So tell me Rosalyn what have you been doing since last we met?' he asked smoothly.

The liar, he did not know her from Adam... Rose wanted to burst out laughing. 'Well let me see,' she murmured, her hand on his shoulder sliding down his arm so she could lean back a little and look directly into his tanned face. 'I got married a week ago.'

'My heart is broken—you should have waited for me. But at least let me kiss the bride.' Before she guessed his intent he puckered up and planted a big sloppy kiss on her cheek. 'Who is the lucky man and I will kill him.' He played the part of wounded suitor to the hilt, his cheeky eyes glittering with fun.

She couldn't stop herself from giggling. 'Sebastian you don't remember me at all. Maylyn, ten years ago,' she prompted. 'Now Mrs—'

She never got to finish the sentence. Sebastian's hands fell from her waist and, for a second she glimpsed a look of sheer terror in his eyes, before he was smiling at someone behind her. Abruptly she was jerked back against a hard body, and twisting her head she looked up into the angry face of Xavier.

'Now my wife. Sebastian.' He wasn't looking at Rose, all his attention was on the other man.

'My heartiest congratulations, old friend. I hope you will both be very happy. I am only sorry I missed the wedding.'

'Well I did not think it was worth calling you back from Buenos Aries before you completed the job. In fact I did not expect you back so soon. How did it go?' The conversation continued in Spanish.

Sebastian must still work for Xavier, she mused, and they were obviously the best of friends, as they both completely ignored her. She lifted her hand to cover Xavier's at her waist. He did not seen to know it but he was squeezing the breath out of her. Her finger slipped under his but he simply squeezed her hand and lifting it to his mouth kissed her fingertips.

'Say goodnight to Sebastian, Rosalyn *querida;* we are leaving.'

Rose looked up at Xavier. Noting the indomitable façade—the polite social smile that gave nothing away. She glanced back at Sebastian. 'Goodnight. It was nice meeting you again.' And it was, she realised as Xavier, still holding her hand, led her through the crowd to the exit. Sebastian had been kind to her when she'd needed it. But as Xavier had said the past was gone, it was all water under the bridge. They could all be friends.

A valet appeared with the car. Xavier took the key and bundling Rose into the passenger seat he slid behind the wheel, and started the engine. The car took off like a bat out of hell.

'Where is the fire?' Rose murmured casting a brief glance at his granite profile.

'Shut up,' he said curtly not taking his eyes from the road.

Which was just as well, Rose thought as the car careered

'round a corner on two wheels. She was beginning to get frightened, and she placed a conciliatory hand on his thigh. 'What happened? Our Host renege on his loan payments or something?' she tried to tease.

He knocked her hand off his thigh and shot her a glance, his face stony. 'Or something.'

'Oh.' She nodded, her gaze intent on his face, his mouth was tight, the hawk-like profile rigid with tension, and then the car took another curve, and she was flung against the passenger door. She stopped worrying about Xavier, her heart in her throat as she glimpsed the sheer drop from the side of the road. She was more concerned about getting home in one piece. It was a journey of pure terror.

The car screeched to a halt inches from the garage door, and Rose leaped out. 'You drove up here like a lunatic. What were you trying to do, kill us both?' It was the relief at standing on firm ground again that made her yell.

Xavier walked around the car and took her arm in a firm grip, almost dragging her up the steps to the door. 'Get in the house before I throw you off the deck,' he said tightly, then pushed her through the hall and into the living room, switching on the light and closing the door behind him as he came after her.

Rose looked at his face and backed away from him. 'What is it, what's the matter?' she whispered, seeing the fierce burning anger in his eyes.

'You dare to ask me that?' Xavier grated lessening the distance between them.

Rose backed away, her green eyes wide and fearful, but she was too slow, his hands reached out, grasping her shoulders, one hand tangling in her hair and jerking her head back viciously. 'One look at Sebastian and you could not help yourself, you were in his arms and kissing him.'

She shook her head. 'No, no, you've got it wrong, Xavier. It wasn't like that.'

'Don't lie to me, damn you,' he roared, his dark eyes leaping with violence.

'I'm not lying to you,' she gasped. He lifted his hand and Rose trembled, closing her eyes waiting for the blow.

'¡Dios mío! What you drive me to.'

Slowly she opened her eyes his arm was arrested in mid-air, his fingers curling in a fist. He looked appalled, and as she watched his hand fell to his side, but his other hand still bit into the flesh of her shoulder.

The transformation from wild fury to ice-cold contempt was frightening to watch. His mouth curved in a chilling smile his dark eyes hard as jet. 'No, I can't blame you. I knew what you were when I married you. The first time we met you left my bed and went straight to Sebastian's. You would have done the same thing tonight if you'd had the chance,' he grated, his lips drawn back against his teeth in a sneer and suddenly he released her with a force that made her stagger.

She raised her head and stared unwaveringly for a moment into his cold accusing eyes. Incredibly he actually believed she'd slept with Sebastian! Finally she understood Xavier's snide comments on her morals and she was rigid with rage. 'I have met Sebastian once before. In *his* flat the morning after you and I made love, the flat you conveniently let me think was your home.'

'I did leave you the key for it, have you forgotten?' he prompted in a maddening drawl.

'How could I. Sebastian told me you kept a bunch to hand out to your lady friends but they didn't fit any known lock,' she said angrily. 'He also told me you were engaged to his sister, and you made a habit of using his apartment for one-night stands, not wanting to sully the honour of your innocent fiancée, an acceptable tradition apparently, in your world.'

He shook his black head slowly in negation. 'I am not so easily fooled. The other day you told me you saw a photograph of my supposed fiancée, now you say Sebastian told you. To be a good liar Rosalyn you need a good memory,' he opined with icy cynicism 'Obviously yours is seriously impaired. Only the other week when I told you I was going to marry you, you admitted you had slept with Sebastian. Something else you have conveniently forgotten?'

Horrified at his assumption she frantically cast her mind back to the day he'd demanded she marry him. At the time she'd been stunned by his proposition but thinking back Xavier had said something about her leaving his bed and falling straight into Sebastian's arms. But it had never entered her head Xavier actually thought she'd had sex with the man.

'I have never ever slept with Sebastian,' she declared adamantly. 'I would not have dreamt of doing such a thing, surely you of all people must know that.' He had been her first lover; he had to know she was telling the truth. 'You *must* believe me.' But one look at his hard mocking eyes told her he did not, and she wondered why she even bothered trying to explain. 'Sebastian did put his arm around me, but on the sofa in the living room.' Xavier's snort of disbelief was audible, and Rose felt like thumping him to knock some sense into his arrogant head. 'And only because he was comforting me after explaining what a louse you were.'

'And that was when you both discovered that you had a sudden passion for each other.'

'Don't be ridiculous.' Rose was suddenly furious and fed up with the whole thing. 'As far as I'm concerned you deceived and deserted me,' she said bitterly, and spun around and began heading for the bedroom, anywhere out of his sight, before she burst into tears. The evening that had started so well was now in tatters.

His hand snaked out and caught her wrist spinning her around to face him. 'Sebastian told me, Rosalyn, and he does not lie. The same as he told me when he telephoned you at your hotel to tell you I had been in a crash, and you informed him you weren't interested.' His lips curved derisively. 'Where was the caring girl then? The girl who is now a *doctor!*' he drawled sarcastically

'You were in an accident the day I left?' she asked, her green eyes widening with horror. 'I never knew.'

'Never cared you mean.'

'No, no, you are wrong. I never spoke to Sebastian after I left the apartment. I left the hotel for the airport after hanging up on you; I was back in England the same night for heaven's sake! Sebastian could not have phoned me even if he wanted to. I honestly never knew you'd been in an accident,' Rose said fiercely 'What ever you think or Sebastian told you, I did not know.' She recalled the flicker of terror in Sebastian's eyes tonight when he finally discovered who she was, and with a flash of blinding clarity the truth dawned. Sebastian had been protecting his sister's interests ten years ago. 'Sebastian lied to you, Xavier.'

'And you expect me to believe you,' he drawled mockingly. His fingers tightening around her wrist in an iron grip. 'I have known Sebastian for years, he's a life-long friend, he would not lie to me.'

'He did,' she contradicted flatly. 'Sebastian never phoned me and I never slept with him,' she tried one last time.

Xavier gave her a caustic cynical smile 'Says you...'

His mocking sarcasm was the final straw. Deeply hurt at his total lack of trust in her, she said in a tight voice. 'Believe what you like.' She shrugged tiredly. 'What difference does it make, you will anyway. Now if you don't mind, let go of my wrist. I'm going to bed.'

'Yes.' He released her wrist, and gave a humourless laugh. 'The best place for a woman like you. Don't worry Rosalyn, whether I believe you or not is immaterial, we are married. I am quite prepared to forget the past and have a go at making the best of what we have got.' And suiting action to his words, his hands enclosed her waist, and drew her towards him.

Rose gave a stifled gasp before his hard mouth covered hers in a blistering ruthless kiss, that only ended when he had her complete capitulation.

Alone in the bedroom, Rose undressed, her green eyes hazed with moisture as she removed the necklace he'd given her a few hours earlier from her throat. From ecstasy to tragedy in one night she thought sadly. But without trust their relationship had no chance none at all. Xavier was never going to believe her above his friend. Then the sickening realisation hit her. If Sebastian had lied to Xavier, it followed he might have lied to her. If she had tried the key that fatal day, if she had spoken to Xavier when he called her at the hotel, asked him outright if he was engaged, if she had trusted him... If was the loneliest word in the English language, and the tears streamed down her cheeks.

It was ten years too late. Xavier was never going to love her as she dreamed of being loved. How long could she stand a marriage based on just physical passion? She climbed into bed and buried her face in the pillow and let the tears fall. She wept as she had never wept since the loss of her baby, and finally, all cried out, she fell into a sleep of utter exhaustion.

IN THE RASH...                                                             171

...eve that you like,' She shrugged lightly. 'What difference
does it make, you will anyway. Now, I you don't mind, let
go of my wrist. You are hurting me.'
...y.   He rele...                                        at flowed as
...   The last place I w...   see you. I say I worry

## CHAPTER ELEVEN

ROSE, her vision blurring with tears stepped forward and
dropped a handful of earth on the coffin. Don Pablo had
been her salvation over the last five weeks and now he was
dead and they were burying him.

On return from her so-called honeymoon they'd moved
into the master suite at the Hacienda and Xavier had treated
her in the same manner as he had before they married:
playing the attentive husband in front of people, but avoiding her all day if he could. It was only at night in the wide
bed that his phenomenal control slipped, and he gave in to
the passion they ignited in each other. But it was not
love...and for the past three weeks it had been nothing at
all as they'd occupied separate bedrooms.

Rose had spent most of her time with Don Pablo, caring
for him, and in return he had been teaching her Spanish.
Two weeks after they'd returned to the Hacienda, Xavier
had gone to Seville for a few days leaving her with his
father. Don Pablo had taken a turn for the worse and Doctor
Cervantes had asked Rose if she would administer the mor-
phine and take charge of the old man's pain control. On
his return from Seville, Xavier had used it as an excuse to
occupy a separate bedroom. Telling her he did not want to
disturb the little sleep she got while looking after his father.
Personally Rose believed it was because he'd taken up with
his mistress again, but she'd never asked him.

Instead she'd got to know and love Don Pablo. He'd
delighted her with stories of Xavier's childhood, and the

night before he died he'd made her promise she would not leave his son. He'd sensed all was not right between them.

A sad smile curved her mouth, as she brushed a tear from her cheek with a trembling hand. She was going to miss the old man. But she had the satisfaction of knowing he had died at peace with her secret revealed to him.

She turned away from the grave and walked back to stand beside Xavier. But there was no supporting arm from her husband. He stood rigid, his emotions held in check, his dark eyes cold as the Arctic waste as they flicked briefly over her, and then returned to contemplate the soil-splattered coffin nestled in the dry earth. Then everyone was moving back to the waiting cars and the drive back from the church to the house.

Circulating among the guests an hour later, Rose was surprised that Don Pablo had so many friends and was held in such high regard that members of the government were in attendance. Glancing around the crowd she checked everything seemed to be in order. Tables laden with food were set out in the courtyard. The champagne flowed freely, all at Don Pablo's specific request. He'd not wanted his friends to weep for him.

A movement to her left drew her attention and turning her head her glance rested on her husband. Xavier stood tall and sombre in a severe black suit, and as she watched his dark head bent towards Isabelle, who was dressed in a tiny slip of a black dress that exposed most of her chest and eighty percent of her legs. She was crying and clinging to Xavier's arm.

A bitter smile curved Rose's mouth. She had thought Xavier had taken up with his mistress again, but perhaps she was wrong, perhaps it was Isabelle if today's display was anything to go by. Suddenly Xavier's head lifted and his dark eyes caught her staring. She raised her brows, her eyes running over him with contempt she did not bother trying to disguise. She saw his mouth tighten in an angry white line. Well, what did he expect? Flirting at his father's funeral. Spinning on her heel she made tracks for the back of the house.

She needed to think, and the relative quiet of the long terraced garden that led down to the lake was the ideal place. She sat down on a strategically placed wooden seat, which had been a favourite of Don Pablo's and stared out over the shimmering blue water. The heat was not quite so intense, with the lush vegetation cascading over from the terrace above providing some shade. She sighed, and smoothed the skirt of her black linen dress down over her knees. She bent her head back, closed her eyes, and slowly rotated her head on her shoulders, trying to ease the tension at the top of her spine. It had been a stressful few weeks. The thought made her groan in disgust. That must be the biggest understatement ever...

'May I join you?'

She opened her eyes. 'Sebastian.' She didn't want to speak to the man, but good manners forced her response. 'If you like.'

He smiled rather warily and moved to sit down beside her, and suddenly something in Rose snapped. She was sick and tired of being polite, playing the part required of her. She was losing her own integrity in the farcical situation of secrets and lies and she'd had enough. She jumped to her feet.

'Yes, I damn well do mind.' She turned on Sebastian, her green eyes clashing angrily with his. 'How dare you tell Xavier all those lies about me? What gave you the right to play God with other people's lives?'

Sebastian flinched. 'So he's told you.'

'What do you expect? He's my husband,' she said

briskly curbing her temper. For her own satisfaction she needed to know exactly what Sebastian had or had not done ten years ago. 'You actually told him I slept with you. How could you?'

'I know. I know and I'm sorry. But you were a stranger to me, and Xavier and I had been friends since childhood, plus he's my employer. I never thought the two of you would meet again.'

At least he had the grace to look ashamed, Rose thought. 'But why?' she asked.

'Can't you guess?' he said wryly. 'You're a stunningly beautiful woman, the minute I saw you in the apartment I knew you were different from all the rest of the girls in Xavier's life, and you were a serious threat. I loved my sister Catia, and she'd wanted Xavier for years.'

'You said they were engaged. You told me she was a virgin, it was tradition. Xavier was honouring her innocence.' With hindsight she realised how dumb it sounded.

A harsh laugh escaped him. 'I wished they were. Catia had slept with Xavier years before, but he'd never taken her seriously, mainly because he was not the first or the last. That week in Barcelona she was hoping to get him back; he was unattached at the time. I was going to help her. But when you walked into the room and showed me that door key I knew I had to get rid of you so I made up the story about him having a bunch to give out to his lady friends. I took a chance you'd be too embarrassed to try, and I won.'

She shook her head in disgust. 'And Xavier's car crash?'

'He crashed on the way to your hotel. I was in the car with him trying to persuade him not to bother. I told him you'd left the key, and had simply said "Thanks and goodbye." He didn't believe me, and then it did not matter because a drunk driver on the wrong side of the road drove into him. Funnily enough Xavier's car was hardly damaged but he got burned pulling the other man out of his car.'

'Oh my God,' Rose whispered. 'And when he came 'round you let Xavier think I knew about his accident but did not want to see him.'

'Yes, the last thing Xavier told me was to call you at the hotel before he lost consciousness.'

'And did you?'

'Yes I did and they told me you had already checked out.' A slight noise in the bushes made Sebastian's head turn. 'What was that?'

'Nothing,' Rose said impatiently. 'So what did you do?'

'I told Xavier you weren't interested.' Sebastian shrugged his broad shoulders. 'You'd believed my story and gone, and Xavier was in hospital for weeks, with Catia playing the devoted girlfriend. It was only three months later when you called me and asked to speak to him that I panicked. He was fit, and talking about contacting you to confront you. I told him he was wasting his time, you were not worth the effort, and to finally convince him I reluctantly admitted I'd made love to you the morning after him.' Rose stared at him with horror filled eyes. The depths of his deception appalled her.

'You have to understand,' he grabbed her arm. 'I had to do it to protect my sister. Xavier was Catia's last chance. There were rumours people were beginning to talk about her.'

'So when I called you, and you rang me back and told me Xavier was getting married the next week, that was a lie as well?' Rose prompted flatly.

'Yes. But after I had told him I had slept with you he did not seem to care anymore, and a couple of months later he married Catia anyway.'

Briefly she closed her eyes. So many lies, the life of a

child and all for what? Glancing back at Sebastian's dark troubled face she asked bitterly. 'Why are you telling me now ten years too late? It can't be your conscience bothering you. You obviously don't have one.'

'I'd like to know the answer to that myself.'

Rose spun around and glanced up in shock at Xavier's thunderous countenance. 'Xavier, what are you doing here?'

He shot her a furious glance, a muscle jerking in his cheek, 'Get back to the house and take care of our guests. I'll take care of this.'

Rose was about to refuse, she looked from one man to the other, Sebastian's expression was defiant, Xavier's face was murderous. They were like two stags at bay, or two chauvinist pigs she thought cynically, who between them had almost destroyed her life once. Rose's stomach curled in disgust at what she'd heard, and with a hardness she had not known she was capable of, she decided to let them destroy each other. What did she care? And with a shrug of her slender shoulders, she brushed past the pair of them, and made her way back to the house.

She took a glass of champagne from a passing waiter, and downed it one go, anger and resentment sizzling inside her. But her rage gave her the strength to mingle with the guests and accept the condolences of Don Pablo's many friends.

'Rosalyn, my dear,' Doctor Cervantes stopped her. 'I'm leaving now, but I could not go without expressing my gratitude once more. Don Pablo was a very lucky man to have you to look after him, and he knew it. Although this is a sad day, Don Pablo would have appreciated it. God rest his Soul. You have done him proud.'

Rose smiled at the old man, who was a little bit the worse

for drink but his sentiment was genuine. 'Thank you, and thank you for coming.'

'No, thank you. I am getting old, too old to run a full-time practice. Later you and I must talk. I need a partner, someone young. Your grasp of the Spanish language is phenomenal under Don Pablo's tutelage, so think about it.'

'I will,' she assured him, flattered by his offer, and wished him goodnight.

The next hour saw most of the guests depart. Rose caught a glimpse of Xavier tall and aloof above the heads of the crowd, but he avoided her eyes. His harsh features were set in a brooding impenetrable mask that most people probably thought was grief, but Rose was not so sure. Her anger had cooled somewhat and the more she thought about Sebastian's revelations the more a tiny seed of hope grew in her heart. If she and Xavier talked honestly and openly with each other, perhaps their marriage could be saved. Then she saw her husband wishing Isabelle goodnight, and she castigated herself for being a naive fool. Nothing had changed... She watched him kiss the woman on both cheeks, and then straighten up and look around. Xavier's dark eyes clashed with Rose's, and she watched him approach with a dull ache in her heart.

'Rosalyn,' he took her elbow. 'It is time we said goodnight to our guests.'

She shrugged his hand off her arm. 'You mean now that Isabelle, your lady friend has left,' she drawled sarcastically.

His black eyes narrowed on her angry face. 'She is not now and never has been my girlfriend as I have told you before,' he said tightly. 'Now will you take my arm and behave as my wife until the last guest has left in deference to my father's memory.'

Put like that she could not refuse, and she stood in the

spacious hall, supremely conscious of the closeness of his tall virile body at her side, the light touch of his hand on her bare arm, until the last goodbye was said. Then she abruptly pulled away and turned to face Xavier to ask the question that had been preying on her mind for the past two hours.

'What happened to Sebastian?'

Xavier stared at her, his face rigid. 'He left and is no longer any concern of yours.'

'I see, and that's all you are going to say?' she asked. He was so coldly controlled and then she noted his hands were curled into fists at his sides, the knuckles of one hand white with strain, but on the other red raw.

'You didn't hit him?' she exclaimed.

'No, I grazed my hand on a wall.' Without looking at her he added, 'Now if you will excuse me it has been a hard day and I still have things to sort out.' And he almost knocked her down in his haste to get past her.

Rose watched the back of his black head, the taut set of his shoulders, as he disappeared into the study and slammed the door behind him, leaving her alone. He knew the truth now, he knew Sebastian had lied to them both and yet he had still walked away from her... He didn't care... Never had...

Face it, she thought bitterly, Xavier did not want her, the passion had burnt out. He hadn't touched her in three weeks. He had vanished most days only returning in the evening to sit with his father, and leaving when Rose entered the sickroom. She saw again his affectionate farewell kiss to Isabelle in her mind's eye. What did it matter whether it was his mistress or Isabelle who he was spending his time with? Xavier had promised her fidelity, and broken the promise.

Rose blinked away the tears that threatened to fall and

glanced around the now empty hall. It was the end of an era she thought sadly. No more Don Pablo and possibly no more Rosalyn Valdespino. She wished she could go back to Dr. May and forget the last few months had ever happened. But life was never that simple. What was a deathbed promise worth? Did one broken promise justify breaking another?

Deeply troubled she wandered through into the kitchen. Max was about to leave for the night and he tried to smile at her as she wished him goodnight, but his face was ravaged by grief. Rose sank down onto a hard-backed chair and leaned her arms on the table, her head drooping. She was so tired and emotionally drained she doubted she had the strength to make it to bed, and she certainly did not have the strength to challenge her husband. She had no idea how long she sat there, but eventually with a heavy sigh and after wiping a few stray tears from her eyes, she headed back to the hall, and then she heard it.

The howl was like the cry of some animal in pain, followed by what sounded like the shattering of glass. It was coming from the study. Without thinking she crossed the hall and pushed open the study door.

Xavier was slumped on the black leather sofa, his head in his hands, his great shoulders shaking. On the terrazzo floor was a discarded jacket and tie and the shattered remains of a bottle, and small pool of amber liquid. The persuasive scent of brandy hung in the air and on the sofa table stood an empty glass.

'Xavier,' she murmured. His iron control had finally cracked and she rushed to sit down on the sofa beside him, and put a consoling arm around his shoulders.

He threw back his head, and turned wet dark brown eyes on her. 'Rosalyn you are still here. Is my torment never to end?' he groaned, pushing unsteady fingers through his tousled black hair.

'Shh… I know. It is all right to grieve, your father was a wonderful man,' she murmured soothingly, her heart full of compassion for this arrogant, usually invulnerable man, brought low by his father's death.

His hand lifted to push back a stray curl from her forehead. 'Your sympathy unmans me,' he said in a roughened tone, his long fingers grasping her chin and tilting her face up to his. 'And I can't lie to you. The death of my father is not my torment. You are,' he declared hoarsely. 'How can you bring yourself to speak to me after the way I have behaved? You must hate me.'

'I'm a doctor, I care for people.' She tried to be flippant but her voice shook as emotion almost choked her. 'And I could never hate you,' was as far as she dared go in revealing her true feelings. She watched him breathe again, watched his dark eyes roam over her face her hair her slender body and back to her face.

Xavier looked long and hard at her, the tension building in the air between them, his hand tightened imperceptibly on her chin. 'But can you ever learn to love me?' he asked hoarsely, and she was stunned into silence by the fear and loneliness she glimpsed in his eyes, knowing the same emotions haunted her.

'No, of course you can't,' he said leaping to his feet. He spun around to stare down at her. 'I forfeited the right to ask when I believed the lies Sebastian fed me,' he grated bitterly. 'When I blackmailed you into marrying me. ¡Dios! I'm amazed you're still here. I was convinced you would take off the minute the funeral was over and the last guest departed. I shut myself in here intending to get drunk so I would not have to see you go.' His strained mouth curved in wry grimace 'I couldn't even get that right. I dropped the bottle.'

Slowly Rose got to her feet, and laid her hand on his arm. 'Do you want me to go?' she asked, feeling her way, her fingers unconsciously stroking his bare forearm.

He looked at her pale hand on his tanned flesh 'No.' She watched the strong cord of his throat move convulsively as he swallowed, 'No. No damn it, I love you, I always have.' Rose heard the words she'd longed to hear and hope blazed in her heart. 'For ten long lonely years, through a sham of a marriage to a woman I did not love and should never have married. And now I have found you again, it is too late—I love you far too much to keep you here against your will.'

She tensed. 'And who would you put in my place, Isabelle or your mistress?' she had to ask, she'd been torn apart the last few weeks imagining him in another woman's arms.

Wild eyes captured hers. 'Never. No one on this earth can take your place Rosalyn. You must know that, you must feel it when I am with you, lost in you, loving you.'

'But for the past few weeks...'

Xavier cut in, 'I have suffered the torture of the damned—burning for you, aching for you, and not daring to touch you. My father adored you, he told me so the night before I went to Seville. He was so happy for me, because I had finally found the perfect woman. In the short time he knew you, he recognised your inner goodness, your caring and compassionate nature, your honesty, and in his mind you were almost a saint. A dying man could see what I refused to see. After our wedding I felt the lowest of the low, not fit to be the dirt beneath your feet because I knew he was right. I didn't need to hear Sebastian confess to his lies, I already knew the things I accused you of could not possibly be true, and I felt such overwhelming love for you and at the same time a terrible guilt. I ran off to Seville for a few days because I could not face what I had done to you.'

'Oh, Xavier,' Rose whispered.

'No, let me finish. When I returned, and watched you with my father, talking, soothing him, caring for him. I was filled with such self-loathing I didn't dare touch you or tell you how much I loved you. I didn't deserve you, but I was terrified you would run away again.'

He would not look her in the eye, but he had said he loved her. She was not going to let him get away with playing the noble man. 'You don't see me running,' she murmured throatily. 'Unless it is to the bedroom.'

His dark head shot back and his dulled eyes, glinting with a golden light, clashed with hers. 'Rosalyn I am putting my heart on the line here, don't joke,' he said tautly, his mouth twisting in a shadowy smile as he admitted, 'I can't bear it.'

Slipping her arm around his neck she leaned into the hard warmth of his body and tipped back her head, her eyes gleaming with a look as old as Eve. 'No joke: I love you.'

Two strong arms wrapped round her like steel bands. 'I don't believe it, but I'm not letting you change your mind. I need you desperately, Rosalyn. I need the sweet solace of your touch tonight. I need to lose myself in the passion of your body, and if this is all a dream I don't care,' he declared raggedly, and took her mouth with a hard raw hunger that spoke for itself.

Then cradling her in his arms they reached the bedroom, and he set her on her feet and quickly freed the buttons down the front of her dress. Her hands were just as mobile, and in seconds they were naked on the bed. His mouth sought her lips, his tongue plunged into the moist dark heat of her mouth with a hungry desperation. Rose wound her arms lovingly around his neck, it seemed like a lifetime since he'd kissed her, and this time when she said, 'I love you' he believed her. After drowning in grief and loss all day, it was a confirmation of love and the continuity of life, a pinnacle of pleasure for the body and a healing balm to the soul.

'What really happened to Sebastian?' she asked a long time later as she lay in his arms, languorous in the aftermath of their lovemaking. She lifted his damaged hand to her mouth and kissed the raw knuckles.

'I think you know,' he drawled mockingly. 'I saw you leave the house and I watched Sebastian follow you. I followed him and heard everything he said to you. I was on the terrace above and I wanted to kill him. He lied to both of us. When I think of the years we have wasted…' Xavier tightened his arms around her and he rubbed his chin against the top of her head. 'But I restrained myself to one punch, and we will never see him again.'

'He is your friend,' Rose murmured. 'And he was looking after his sister.'

'He was my friend.' Xavier said trenchantly. 'But some things in life are unforgivable.' He turned her in his arms, and caught her chin, a wry smile slanting his lips, 'Though I have not asked your forgiveness for my despicable behaviour.' The thought made him frown. 'In fact it was all my fault,' he swore angrily. 'I knew I should have looked for you.'

'You had a terrible accident, and yet according to Sebastian you were still going to. That is good enough for me, you're forgiven, and anyway it as much my fault. I should not have believed the lies he told either.'

'You were only nineteen. I was years older and should have known better,' he said, a rueful smile replacing the frown. 'Only one thing puzzles me. What made you ring Sebastian three months after you had left?'

Rose had been dreading the question but she could not avoid it. Her green eyes shadowed with pain. 'I discovered I was pregnant a month after I returned to England. I had my apartment and enough money, and I told myself I would be fine as a single mother. Aunt Jean thought I was on a holiday so I had no need to tell anyone. But I knew you had a right to know, and as the weeks went by I began to get more and more depressed on my own, and finally I rang the number on the card you gave me and spoke to Sebastian. I did not tell him I was pregnant, simply that it was urgent I speak to you, though I think he might have guessed. Anyway he called me back and said you did not want to speak to me, and you were getting married the next week.' Rose stopped and glanced up at Xavier his handsome face was expressionless.

'Go on.'

Suddenly she realised he thought she'd got rid of their child. 'I be...began to bleed that same day,' she stammered. She still found it terribly upsetting to talk about. 'I was rushed into hospital that night and suffered a miscarriage; stress or shock, or perhaps it was just not meant to be...'

'No. ¡Dios! No.' Xavier cried out. 'If I'd known that I would have killed the bastard.'

'It's all right.' Her hands lifted to cradle his hard cheekbones 'It was a long time ago and over now.'

'No, it is not.' Her heart bled for the anguish in his face. 'You don't understand I was married for eight years, we rarely made love, but for some reason Catia never conceived. Maybe my chances of fathering a child are slim, and now you tell me we lost one. The one argument between my father and I was my failure to provide an heir.'

'Well, if your father is looking down on us now,' Rose

said gently smoothing the frown lines across his broad brow with her fingers, 'He will have a broad grin on his loveable old face. Maybe I should have told you first but I told your father the night before he died, and it made him very happy. I'm pregnant.'

'You're carrying my child.' Xavier's voice was deep and rough, his stunned glance sweeping down over the length of her naked body. One hand roamed possessively down over her breast and settled on the flat plain of her stomach, his dark eyes shinning with an adoring glow. 'You're sure? When—'

Rose grinned. 'I am a doctor, and the Valdespino tradition of the harem bed is still working.'

'The first night,' he said. 'Both times.' And a smile of pure masculine complacency split his dark face. She had her handsome arrogant husband back.

Reaching up Rose threaded her fingers through his hair; glad she'd banished the doubt about fatherhood from his mind. She pulled his head down to her waiting lips. 'Want to play Doctor and Nurse?'

'With me as the nurse,' he said drolly.

'Xavier there are male nurses, your chauvinism is rising again.'

'It's not the only thing,' he growled and his husky chuckle and the kiss that followed was long and tender, tinged with regret, forgiveness asked, forgiveness granted, and a soaring passionate promise for the future.

This Christmas, experience
the love, warmth and magic that
only Harlequin can provide with

*Mistletoe*
*Magic*

a charming collection from

# BETTY NEELS
## MARGARET WAY  REBECCA WINTERS

*Available November 2000*

HARLEQUIN®
*Makes any time special*™

Visit us at www.eHarlequin.com

PHMAGIC

# Coming in October 2000

HARLEQUIN®
AMERICAN ROMANCE®

brings you national bestselling author

# ANNE STUART

## with her dramatic new story...

*A man untamed, locked in silence.*
*A woman finally ready to break free.*

*Available at your favorite retail outlet.*

HARLEQUIN®
*Makes any time special* ™

Visit us at www.eHarlequin.com.

HARWT

New York Times
bestselling author

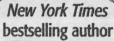

is back with a
brand-new installment in
the breathtaking
**Crighton family saga.**

# COMING
# HOME

*On sale October 2000*

*Makes any time special* ™